CHRISTMAS AT THE OLD BOOKSHOP

A HOLLOWAY GREEN SWEET ROMANCE

AUGUSTA ST. CLAIR

CHRISTMAS AT THE OLD BOOKSHOP

A HOLLOWAY GREEN SWEET ROMANCE

AUGUSTA ST. CLAIR

Christmas at the Old Bookshop: A Holloway Green Sweet Romance
by Augusta St. Clair

Book cover design provided by Bookcoverzone.com.

Thank you so much for supporting this work. Please visit https://augustastclair.wixsite.com/books for more information about Augusta St. Clair's books.

❀ Created with Vellum

For Jane

CHAPTER 1

*A*llison peered down at the elaborate lights and displays lining Fifth Avenue, in shopfronts far below her office window. The holidays in New York could be a magical place, if you weren't chained to a desk.

Unfortunately, Allison had barely had time to breathe since the beginning of December. Jerry, her boss at Regal House Books (a wholly owned subsidiary of Bartleby-Flores-Bergman International Publishing, Inc.), had been piling tasks onto her relentlessly. This had been going on for weeks now, as Jerry tried to cram in as much work as possible before the company-wide Christmas break.

"O'Brien," someone said crisply behind her. "You're not really leaving the *state* for Christmas, are you?"

She glanced back at the slightly grey-faced man who'd followed her into the conference room. Jerry was a Manhattan native. He wouldn't even need to leave the island to spend time with his extended family for Christmas. Like many lifelong New Yorkers, he had trouble with the concept of a world existing outside the five boroughs, never mind whole other states.

"My family's in rural New Hampshire," she said, wondering if her explanation would sink in this time. "They run a ski area."

"*Rural* New Hampshire. Is there any other kind?" Jerry fiddled with a battered figurine of Rudolph that someone had smuggled into the midst of far more tasteful decorations arranged on the table by the wall. He shook his head and plucked the Rudolph from the table, then tossed it into the wastebasket. "What if I need you for a last-minute project?"

"Then I'll just come back," Allison said, trying to stifle her annoyance. "I'll be in New England, not Outer Mongolia." She hadn't taken a vacation for some time; frequently her boss made her feel guilty for even insinuating that she wanted to. She'd thought the "mandatory" vacation time meant that she wouldn't have to put up a fight for it, for once. She'd already made plans with Peter to bring him up with her, to meet her family...

"Sorry, Jerry, I just want to ask. This Christmas break is legitimate, right? Not, like, something they say we can have, but we're not really supposed to use?"

"Of course it's legitimate. Mr. Harding wants everyone to have enough time to refresh their brains this time. Then we can hit the ground running in the new year." Her boss gave her a priggish nod.

Good. Finally. She considered asking about the associate editor position that had been vacated recently—but then Allison held the question back. She didn't feel like running into the glass ceiling again right before going on vacation.

When she came back, she could try tackling that particular challenge one more time. Though she didn't have much hope of getting further than she had during her previous attempts at advancement.

"Sounds great," Allison said. "I hope you have a wonderful time off with your family. Are you planning on doing any..."

But Jerry had already turned his back on her and was walking out of the conference room. "Have a great trip," he cast back over his shoulder.

She picked up the mug containing the cold remains of her coffee and returned to her desk—it was just about time to close up shop. Freedom, at last! And she had the perfect activity already scheduled to kick off that freedom: meeting for an early dinner at Le Purloin with her boyfriend, Peter.

The restaurant was several blocks away, but Allison had some time to kill and she wanted to shake off the bad mood Jerry had induced. So she walked along Fifth Avenue, her breath frosting in the cold, allowing herself to dream of home. Everything was less complicated in Holloway Green. And more authentic. Here, the elaborate window displays in the high-end shops, with their constellations of lights and unsettling mannequins modeling two-hundred-dollar sweaters, seemed hopelessly artificial.

Le Purloin was rated a Michelin star, and a current obsession of New York elite thanks to its cutting-edge French-Malaysian fusion cuisine. Soft yellow illumination from the hanging globe lights bathed the hushed, mirror-filled space. Across the dining room, she recognized a popular Broadway actress enjoying a meal. Normally Le Purloin required at least a month to make a reservation, but Allison's boyfriend had pulled some strings. He was good at that.

She found Peter waiting at a table near the front. He stood and greeted her with a rather distant smile, not offering a hug, his eyes dark and tired under his gelled hairline. She and Peter were the same height. Nearly the same weight, too; Peter was rail thin, as if his daily schemings on Wall Street sucked away not just his mental energy but also the meat off his bones. But his angular handsomeness still drew her in.

"How are you, Allison?"

"It's been a day," she said. She didn't elaborate. From the way his gaze wandered, she could tell already that he wasn't listening. And that was fair—she did complain about work a lot. Maybe he was sick of it. So instead, she said, "How was the market today?"

"Oh, a total rollercoaster," her boyfriend said. "You should have seen the traders going crazy..." He became more animated as he spent a solid half an hour telling Allison all about the ups and downs of that particular market day, barely stopping for breath and to tell the server his order. His wine glass was full, and he left it untouched.

Allison gulped down some wine herself. It'd make the dull topic of conversation—monologue?—go somewhat easier. But she played along, seizing any microsecond of pause that she could to offer a supportive reaction.

Right after Peter wound down on the Wall Street discussion, the sense of distance between them grew once more. He became silent as the meal went on. Allison tried not to be deterred by his one-word responses, but eventually she gave up and joined the silence.

As they broke through the crust of the crème brûlée they were sharing, Peter gave her a smooth smile and said, "This isn't working for me anymore."

"No problem—I could totally eat this whole thing myself," Allison said.

He leaned forward, his smile never slipping as he said, "I mean... us. You and me. It's no longer working. On a deep level."

She recoiled as if he'd just slapped her. She could no longer taste the sweet custard, and gulped it down with some difficulty. Her heart picked up a hammering pace.

"No longer *working*? Could you be more specific?" she said.

Peter shrugged. He still seemed so calm, which added to the affront.

"I can't believe this is happening," Allison said numbly. "You're breaking up with me? *Now?*"

"Well," Peter said, "I didn't want to do it during dinner."

Allison blinked at him. *How can he be so obtuse?* "No," she said, "I mean—during the holidays! It's almost Christmas. I…"

She bit her lip, glancing around the restaurant. All these people. She wouldn't let herself cry in front of them. And he'd known that, the jerk. His calm certainty almost tempted her to make a big fuss anyway, just to spite him. That Broadway actress wasn't the only one here who could make a scene.

"Would you really rather I'd waited until January?" Peter said patiently. "All that pretending I'd have to do with your family over the holidays, that wouldn't be fair to them, would it? It wouldn't be fair to you, either."

"Oh, you're a real humanitarian." He did have a point, though, and that stung her too. What if he'd dumped her right *after* the holidays? She might have even blamed her poor parents and siblings for saying something "wrong" to him. *If I'm being honest with myself, I'd be the last one I'd blame…*

Peter shrugged. "I wish it didn't have to be this way," he said with patent insincerity. "But, you know. It is what it is."

After all the attention she'd given him over the past year, devoting her precious free time to him when she was so tired from the demands of her job, it just wasn't fair. More than that, it didn't make sense… something was missing.

Peter's eyes were cold. For a minute she couldn't even fathom what she'd ever seen in him. Such cold eyes—had they ever been warm, or had she just been distracted by his good looks?

"Relationships don't end just like that," Allison said. "Give me a *reason*. Is there someone else?"

"No," Peter said.

She could tell he was lying, by the way he fidgeted, by the way he held himself.

"Come on, Peter," Allison said. *"Please."*

"All right," he said finally. "It's Julie. From work. We've been dating for a couple of months now. I never meant to hurt you, Allison." His eyes gave away the emptiness of his words. Even if he'd "never meant" to hurt her, he sure hadn't made any effort to stop himself from doing so. Repeatedly. That, more than anything, twisted the dagger into Allison's heart.

"Julie," she said. She said it again before the word meant anything at all to her. She'd met the woman once or twice, had never given her a second thought. Right now she couldn't even picture what this Julie looked like, and that was probably for the best.

She started to ask Peter *why*—why he would do this to her. Why he was attracted to Julie... why he was no longer attracted to Allison. Why he thought he could simply gloss over that information and get away with a simple breakup. Why he had let her sit through a whole dinner with him, like a fool, rather than breaking up with her the moment he saw her tonight.

But the single syllable died on her lips... as she realized she didn't care about the answers to any of those *why*s. None of it mattered, did it?

This was over.

"I hope you'll consider still being friends," he said, rotely.

"I hope you'll consider jumping in the East River," Allison said numbly. She got up from the table and walked away, with poise, not allowing herself to break down until she was well out of view of Le Purloin. Then the sobs hit her with violent force, until she thought she was going to be sick.

ALLISON MET her younger sister Christine in the baggage area of the Manchester airport, an hour and a half south of Holloway Green. Her sister had rejected Allison's plan to take a rental car from the airport, insisting on driving down to pick her up instead.

"Hey! Allie!"

Christine jumped up and down at the sight of Allison. Definitely much cheerier than the last time Allison had seen her… which was when? That couldn't have been six months ago already, could it? Allison swallowed. Then she started laughing as she took in the sight of Christine's outfit.

Her sister wore an oversized, puffy winter coat with a huge fur hood that had to be twice the size of Christine's head. It was open to reveal camo patterning on the inside lining. Underneath, Christine was wearing an "ugly Christmas sweater"—the theme of this one was dinosaurs in Santa hats.

"Chris," Allison gasped. Her laughter had gotten out of control. "What… why?"

"Wanted to make sure you could spot me," Christine said cheerfully.

Then she burst into a fit of giggling too. The sisters wrapped their arms around each other in a bear hug. Allison had to stop laughing before it turned into a maudlin sob. She took a deep breath and got herself to calm down.

"Ah man," she murmured into Christine's shoulder, "I'm guessing our dear brother gave you that sweater."

"Yep. Though it's from last year. You totally missed out— you could have gotten one too." Christine pulled away and gave Allison a careful, exaggerated inspection. Her glittering blue eyes, so much like Allison's own, traveled up and down Allison's new cashmere coat.

"Well, look at you!" she said. "You've gotten even more stylish since this summer. I hate to break it to you, but we're all wearing dino sweaters in Holloway Green these days. You're going to stick out like a sore thumb."

That was the last thing Allison wanted. Christine had been joking, of course, but what if Allison really did stand out in her little hometown—and not in a good way? *I don't want them all to think I've grown into a snob. Worse, a New York City snob.* She fingered the collar of her coat, suddenly nervous. "I'll do my best to blend in."

Christine cocked her head, probably curious at the change in Allison's mood. She gave Allison her trademark impish grin and said, "Nah! Don't! You could make a little Manhattan wear off onto Holloway Green."

"That stubborn town?" Allison said, shrugging. "I wouldn't count on it. Remember the fight over the Main Street traffic light?"

Her sister looked thoughtful then. "True enough. Some things never change, even when they should. Reminds me… anyway, let me grab your bag. Which one is it?"

Halfway into the drive home, as Route 16 north wound through the darkness of the vast New Hampshire forests, traffic tightened. Cars slowed, and eventually Christine's little lavender coupe found itself snarled in a full-on jam. Allison turned down the radio; the Christmas music now seemed a little too relentless and repetitive.

"Where are they all going?" she said, squinting out the window at the endless red taillights ahead of them.

"Home for the holidays, same as you," Christine said, drumming her fingers on the dash. "Just be glad you don't have to be heading south out of Holloway Green on

8

Christmas night, when everyone in the universe is heading back to Manch or Massachusetts. Total standstill."

"*This* is a standstill."

"Nah, just give it a minute," Christine said.

She realized she had nowhere to be in a hurry, for once. It felt good. She stretched her travel-weary limbs and asked, "Did Mom and Dad turn my old bedroom into an office?"

"Nope, still a shrine to the prodigal daughter. They turned *my* bedroom into an office. Like, I'll have to fold out the couch every night."

"You're not staying at your own place?" Allison asked, curious.

"No, it's a little... it'll be more fun to have all of us in the same house for the holidays," her sister said. "It'll be like old times. Sam, he's still living in the basement, of course. To be close to Jackpine, he says."

Allison nodded, though she was thinking about how Christine lived all of five minutes from their parents' house. Probably her sister felt lonely in her own house, rattling around by herself, especially at Christmastime. "It will be fun."

"Hey, by the way, I'm sorry Peter couldn't make it up here with you. We were all excited to meet him."

She winced. She hadn't had the heart to tell Christine, or the rest of the family, about the breakup yet. Now wasn't the right time, either. She didn't want to have to rehash the story to each individual family member. So she said, "Ah yeah, he's a busy guy, but he sends his best."

Then she quickly changed the subject: "How have things been going at Jackpine Mountain?"

Christine hesitated. "Oh, you know. Fine."

That didn't sound promising. Allison had left the family business to pursue her own career, but of course she still cared about it and fretted over it from time to time. A ski area took a lot of effort and creative problem-solving to maintain. She'd set up alerts to send her e-mails every time there was a news story that mentioned Jackpine Mountain. "Fine?"

"I feel like the tourist and recreation business isn't quite what it used to be," Christine said. "I mean, Jackpine is still seeing good business. People are still coming up. But not as many as there should be, thanks to the tough economy."

"Hm. Do you think downtown has been taking a hit too? Are they still running the horse-drawn carriages and all the other holiday stuff?"

"They're definitely in a downturn. Struggling. The mayor and the town council don't seem to have a plan for recovery, so everyone's scrambling to save themselves. It's been like this for a while. Did you know The Old Bookshop had to close earlier this year?"

Allison shook her head in dismay. A flood of fond memories hit her, most of them revolving around the funny, kindly proprietor whom most of the town referred to as "Grandpa Skip." He did act as a grandfather to generations of kids, fostering a love of reading at a young age. Allison would have never gotten interested in the book publishing business were it not for him. She'd decided, early in her life, that she wanted to help put together the kind of books she saw on the shelves of The Old Bookshop.

"Ah, that's awful!" she said. "I love that place. Is Skip Whitfield okay?"

"Fine, I think," Christine said, "but Grandpa Skip could probably use a visit from you while you're here. Do you think you could squeeze that in?"

"Of course," Allison said. "So, did he just run out of money? Didn't the town try and put together a fundraiser? The Old Bookshop is an institution, not to mention the man himself..."

"Like I said, the town leadership doesn't seem to care that Holloway Green is falling apart all around them," her sister said. "And most folks are struggling to stay afloat themselves."

She still couldn't believe it. The Old Bookshop, gone… "Did Grandpa Skip sell it?"

"Not yet. Ben has been helping his grandpa fix it up. He's working at the hardware store, so I think he gets a discount on supplies."

Allison's heart skipped. "Ben Whitfield's back in town? I thought he was off who knows where, rebuilding houses wrecked by hurricanes or something."

"Oh, no, he's been living back in Holloway Green for a year or two now." Christine gave her an innocent smile. "Maybe you should check in with Ben too. I'm sure he'd love to see you."

Allison blushed. She'd had a crush on Ben Whitfield in high school, though the upperclassman had been oblivious to it. He was broad-shouldered and spiky-haired (fashionable for the time), with warm brown eyes revealing the softness behind his strapping exterior… how could she not fall for him? How could anyone avoid drawing his name in their notebooks? But she'd been one of the tallest girls in her grade, nerdy and gangly and awkward—hardly a magnetic presence like he was. Whenever she attempted to talk to him, her nerve had always failed her.

"I'll catch up with Grandpa Skip," she said, "but I'm sure Ben doesn't even remember me."

"Doesn't remember you?" Christine protested. "He asks about you all the time!"

"No way," Allison said.

Christine shrugged. "Okay. Maybe not *all* the time. But he definitely did once."

The cars ahead of them finally started to move. Christine whooped. "Yes! Home sweet home, here we come!"

As the knots of traffic loosened, the O'Brien sisters sped north. The snow piled alongside the highway grew heavier as they reached the White Mountains region. Allison considered asking Christine about whether she'd been brave enough to dip her toe in the proverbial dating pool yet, but ultimately thought better of it. Talk of relationships and love would inevitably lead to probing questions about Peter.

Then, finally, they entered the outskirts of Holloway Green, and Allison's heart lightened.

The town was nestled in the valley between Jackpine Mountain and a couple of other nearby peaks, an oasis of Christmas cheer emerging from the rural darkness. Along the downtown streets—which looked much as they had a hundred years ago, with old-fashioned iron-wrought lamp-posts and brick walkways and storefronts—lighted garlands hung from the snow-dusted trees. Ribboned wreaths adorned the doorways and ringed the street lamps, and potted shrubs along the sidewalks bristled with their own legions of tiny lights. The white tower of Town Hall, looming in a floodlight, balanced the twenty-five-foot Christmas tree glowing on the opposite side of the street.

By night, anyway, it was hard to discern signs of the financial struggle Christine had told her about. The sight of Holloway Green lighting their way with festive abandon made only one word echo in Allison's mind:

Home.

CHAPTER 2

*B*en Whitfield stepped back and surveyed the wooden walls and ceiling of The Old Bookshop with a critical eye. "Grandpa Skip, are you *sure* you don't want me to put in some insulation? The wind is practically whistling through this place. You've probably been losing hundreds of dollars each month just to climate control."

"If you cover the walls with insulation and drywall, people won't be able to see the old woodwork," his grandfather said.

Ben rubbed his chin, feeling stubble coming in. He had helped to build and repair houses in communities stricken by poverty and natural disasters all around the country. During those years, not once had he run into a property owner so stubborn, so resistant to change, as Grandpa Skip. "You can put new wooden panels over the drywall that look like the old ones."

"*New* ones," Grandpa Skip scoffed. "Mr. Ben, you're missing the point. That original woodwork is part of this building's history! It's been standing since the 1860s, since

Holloway Green was just a scrappy little artists' colony and this was a general store. You don't want to go covering up history."

"Well," Ben said, "the less of that kind of 'history' you have on display here, the easier this building'll be to sell." He stole a quick glance at his grandfather. "Again, not that I'm pushing you to sell it. Are you *sure* you want to give up the bookstore? People around here see it as a local institution."

The old man shrugged. He still stood strong and tall despite his age, with a white Van Dyke beard to match his tufted hair. "I don't want to end my days institutionalized. I've put in my fair share of time here, and it's been good years... good decades! But people aren't reading anymore, or not like they used to. The bookselling business is a losing game."

"I don't believe that," Ben said. He took a deep breath. *Here I go with the pitch again.* "I think you just hit a bad couple of years. Listen, what if we looked at these renovations not as preparation for selling the business, but for a grand reopening? I could help you run the shop. I've been reading a lot of books about innovations in managing small businesses that have cropped up in the last decade, with new technol—"

"Not this again," Grandpa Skip grunted, waving Ben's words away. "I won't let you waste your time with this. How'd you get even more sentimental about this musty old place than I am, anyway?"

"I've always loved The Old Bookshop, Grandpa Skip. Holloway Green wouldn't be the same without it."

The old man peered over his glasses at Ben, his mouth creasing in skepticism. "Correct me if I'm wrong. But I thought you spent so long traveling with that Habitat organization because you didn't have an ounce of sentimentality for this town. Or anything in it."

The mention of Ben's time away stung. He tried to

conceal the guilt he was feeling, for running from his surviving family—because he couldn't face the memory of those who were gone. "Came back, didn't I?"

In truth, sentimentality was what had brought Ben back. He'd dreamed of Holloway Green often... the farther Ben's humanitarian missions had taken him across the country, the more he yearned for the place where he'd grown up. The town grew and brightened in his memory, while the shadows left by his parents receded. Grandma dying had been the final catalyst for him to return home, to be close to Grandpa Skip and Ben's sister and niece, but his heart had reopened to New Hampshire long before that.

"You did," Grandpa Skip said softly. "Of course you did. You were there for your grandmother's final days. And for me. I'm sorry, I misspoke." He sighed. "Speaking of your grandmother, I know Helen would agree with you, that I shouldn't offload this place, but—I'm darned tired, Mr. Ben. Tired of fighting a losing battle."

Ben began to object again, but his grandfather held up a hand. "And I'm plain old tired too," he went on. "I could use a rest. I don't get much from Social Security. Selling this place could allow me to be a little more at ease. I can't rely on them throwing me a free hot dog down at the diner every time I show up."

"I dunno," Ben said, grinning, "I think you're on the complimentary Desjardins' Dog list for life. Darleen's always been sweet on you."

Grandpa Skip scoffed. Then the bell over the door rang, and a tall, gorgeous woman walked into the store without hesitation. "Hi," she said. "Sorry to barge in."

"Store's closed, ma'am," said Ben. He was attempting not to stare openly at her, so at first he didn't recognize her. Then, with a shock, he did.

Gawky Allison O'Brien, always with her nose buried in a thick book, even while walking the school hallways...

How long had it been since he'd seen her? Surely he'd run into her sometime since they'd both graduated from their regional high school. But, no, if he had, he wouldn't be this flabbergasted right now.

Allison had... blossomed. That was the only word for it he could think of, the only word that seemed appropriate. Her full lips curved into an amused smile as she watched him struggle with the revelation of knowing her. She was graceful and elegant in a long, cranberry cashmere coat and a patterned scarf winding around her slender neck, with shining dark hair falling to her shoulders and her bright blue eyes even more intense than he remembered. She looked *confident,* a stark contrast from the half-shadowed girl in his memories.

In truth, he had always suspected that the lanky, shy girl at school would grow into a beautiful woman—and that her keen intelligence would earn her great success, whatever she chose to do. He had heard, too, about her landing a job at one of the big book publishing conglomerates in New York. But the sight of her now remained... startling.

Ben had never quite gotten to know Allison, apart from her academic reputation at school. He'd tried a time or two, but she'd always found an excuse to run away just a few sentences into the conversation. He graduated two years ahead of her and then didn't give her, or anyone else in Holloway Green, much thought during his long years of self-imposed exile.

"Allison," he whispered.

"Yes," she said. Her playful smile faltered, revealing a ghost of hesitation. "You remember me. Wow. I definitely remember *you*, Ben Whitfield. You've—grown. You..."

Then she pulled herself back into her former, imposing

stature, and turned her attention to Ben's grandfather. Like so many other Holloway Green kids whose minds had been nourished by The Old Bookshop, she regarded him as an honorary relative: "Grandpa Skip!"

She opened her arms to him, but the old man stayed where he was. Allison protested, "Give me some sugar already!"

Grandpa Skip chuckled. "You, young lady, have been away for too long. When was the last time you actually visited your hometown for Christmas?"

"Aw, I barely ever get any time off. I got lucky this year."

"Still. You'll have to earn my affection back."

"I fully intend to," Allison said. "That's the reason I'm here, Grandpa Skip. I wanted to ask… why in the world would you shut this place down?"

"That's what *I've* been asking," Ben said.

She ignored him. Grandpa Skip replied, "It was all over but the shouting, Allie. Business was becoming unsustainable —sign of the times, I think. Time to pass the torch to someone else… someone who'll pay me for this darned place, that is." He chuckled.

Allison's dark eyebrows knitted. "It should certainly be worth a decent amount. In the right hands, The Old Book-shop could… well, have you had any offers?"

"Not yet," Grandpa Skip admitted, "but I don't blame them for holding back on an as-is sale. I'm sure the hordes will come thundering to my doorstep once we're done sprucing this place up. That's where my hulking young grandson comes into play. Now, you two were in the same class in high school, weren't you?"

"No," Ben said, taking the chance to break into the conversation. "I was two years ahead of her. But I had heard of her just the same. Allison was the biggest brain in the school. Of course, she wouldn't have had the time or inclination to talk to a slacker like me."

"What!" she said indignantly. "I talked to you. Or… well, tried to."

"You'd say hi and then run away," he said. He'd meant to simply tease her with the memory, but now he found himself retroactively ticked off at the way she'd treated him back then; his tone became harder. "I figured I must be pretty dull. Not worth your time, when you were going places."

"No, that's not it," Allison said.

"Then what was it?" Grandpa Skip put in politely, though his attention was really focused on wiping the dust off a nearby bookshelf.

Allison glanced at Ben, then looked away again. Her expression became neutral. "I was an awkward kid, that's all. Don't worry, I've gotten over it."

She wasn't… interested in me back, then, was she? That hardly mattered now. She'd never be interested in him in the present day. She was a big deal in New York, while he was just a small-town hardware store employee fixing up a defunct family business.

"You've been in—New York City, we hear?" Grandpa Skip asked. "Working at one of the Big Six publishers, is that right?"

"Big Five," Allison said. "The big corporate houses are merging together all the time. Pretty soon it'll just be one gigantic company. Who knows if I'll still have a job then!"

Ben wrinkled his forehead, picturing her in the bustle of New York, likely rubbing shoulders with household names. Did she have a guy back in the city? Someone she'd met while at a fancy party in someone's penthouse or something?

Probably.

He shook his head, impatient with his own childish mental wanderings. So what if Allison was with someone?

Even if she weren't, she'd still be headed back to the big city as soon as Christmas was in the rearview.

Interrogating that empty space inside himself only produced the faintest ache. He'd made his own choice long ago to shut himself off from the possibility of romance, shying away from all but the most superficial relationships during his years traveling to aid missions. When he finally returned to Holloway Green, he'd found that basically everyone in town had already paired up with someone. It was just as well.

"What's your job like?" he asked her.

"It's nothing special," she said hastily. "When I get to work with authors directly, the job feels rewarding. Meaningful. But those opportunities are, um, infrequent. I'm just a glorified go-fer most of the time. That's life as an assistant editor."

"Sounds special to me," Ben said with a smile. "You get to work on books, and books are special. Do you help... decide which books your publisher takes on?"

She shrugged. "Only in the most marginal sense. Maybe if I were an associate editor."

"I thought you... oh, you said you were an assistant editor."

"Right. Very different." Allison bit her lip, her brilliant eyes flicking to the floor; she seemed embarrassed. She turned her back on him and went to browse the shelves. All of Grandpa Skip's books were still in place, except for a few moved around during the renovations. He was hoping to sell the property with all of the book stock included in the sale.

"Grandpa Skip," she said, "what are you going to do in your retirement?"

"Well, I've already started doing it," said the old man. "Fixing up old model train sets. Making them pretty again. Building new sets. If I get enough money from the sale of the store to refurbish the RV, maybe I'll take it out on a cross-country adventure like Helen and I used to do. If not, guess I'm not going anywhere!"

Just let me have a go at the business, Ben thought, frustrated. *I'll sell enough books that you can travel around the world.* He didn't want to have the same fruitless argument with Grandpa Skip in front of Allison, but he did feel compelled to break in with *something.* "The Old Bookshop is worth a lot more than a thirty-year-old RV," he said. "Some of us can see that more clearly than others."

Grandpa Skip shot him a look of warning. Ben gritted his teeth. Yes, the fate of the bookstore was definitely his grand-father's decision in the end—his decision alone—but surely Ben couldn't be the only one noticing how much Grandpa Skip was undervaluing the place. He glanced at Allison, hoping she would back him up.

She did—but not in the way he expected.

"Maybe I could help you find a buyer," Allison said. "One that'd *definitely* give you what this place is worth, or more."

What? "How would you do that?"

She darted her blue eyes at Ben and then answered Grandpa Skip, as if he were the one who'd spoken. "I have connections with a lot of booksellers in New York. And bookseller wannabes. I can think of at least two people off the top of my head who have, like, rhapsodized to me about leaving the hectic city life and running a bookstore out in the peaceful countryside."

No! Ben held his tongue and pretended to be interested in the stairs leading to the loft. He leaned on the first step and it provided the audible protest he himself was unwilling to make, squeaking like a mad rodent. Allison jumped at the sound.

"Oh…" Grandpa Skip said. He sounded caught between hope and wariness. "A savior from the Big Apple. That would be an unforeseen ending to this story. If you'd like to, go ahead and ask those *rhapsodizers*. But don't waste too much time on such things. It's Christmas and I'm sure you'll want to spend as much time with your family as you can, rather than running errands for foolish old men."

"I can do both," Allison said brightly. "Believe it or not, I'll need an occasional break from the holiday cheer at Casa O'Brien. It's a full house there with my brother living in the basement and my sister on 'vacation' from her own place until New Year's."

"If you say so. Spiked egg nog may be a more effective escape." Grandpa Skip paused. "Just... please don't send any big-city folks sniffing around here to turn the bookstore into a, a latte factory or something."

Allison looked appalled. "I'd never. The Old Bookshop needs to stay a bookshop."

"Well, good," Grandpa Skip replied, but he still sounded doubtful.

Ben shook the wooden railing of the loft stairs. It had far more give than it should. *That's next on my list.* "Grandpa Skip's right," he said, maintaining a casual tone. "You shouldn't trouble yourself."

"It's no trouble," she said firmly. He glanced back and saw her intense eyes fixed on him, challenging him to offer another objection, just one more.

He smiled politely at Allison. "If Grandpa *had* to sell The Old Bookshop to someone, I think it'd be best to find a *local* buyer. Someone who understands the Holloway Green way of life, who won't try to change the character of the book-store. We don't need this town turning into New York, right?"

Allison snorted. "I don't think there's any danger of that. But could it use a little life breathed into it? Quite possibly."

Grandpa Skip folded his arms. "Blasphemy." He didn't sound like he was joking.

"I'm just saying," Allison said. "Looking around the downtown, it's definitely seen better days."

"There's been an economic downturn," Ben said defensively. "Across the whole country. It's not Holloway Green's fault."

The old man gazed out a grimy front window. "Allison has a point, Mr. Ben. Maybe Holloway Green has been resting on its laurels for too long—it ought to be able to weather the tough times better than this. Either got to get with the times, or step quietly to the side."

"I didn't mean it like that, Grandpa Skip," Allison said. "I want to see this town survive and thrive. I loved growing up here. Just, being away as much I've been, I'm seeing it with fresh eyes."

Ben's grandfather nodded with a faint smile. But Ben had swallowed enough of Allison O'Brien's condescension for one afternoon. *Girl forgets where she comes from.* "Did you need anything else?" he said curtly.

Allison's bright eyes hooded. "No, I suppose I don't." She paused on her way out, the bell jingling above her head. "Grandpa Skip, I'll be in touch after I talk to my city contacts."

"Thank you," Grandpa Skip said. "But again, don't trouble yourself too much…"

She was gone. Ben leaned on the window frame and watched his old classmate stride away. "What is her problem, anyway?"

"She offered to help," his grandfather said. "That's not a problem, that's a potential solution."

It's a problem if it means you sell the bookstore to an outsider, and I never even get a chance.

He helped his grandfather out with a few more minor repairs around the bookstore, though Grandpa Skip continued to refuse touching anything that he deemed "history." That, unfortunately, included the wooden railing along the stairway to the loft. ("The tree that was taken from is no longer with us, thanks to the tragic lightning strike of 1952," Grandpa Skip said. "That's the only piece of the Founders' Tree still in existence—we can't just take it down!")

Finally, feeling cranky and tired, Ben parted from Grandpa Skip for the day and headed out of the store. The reflection of the bright sun on the snow momentarily blinded him. When he regained his vision and lowered his hand, he noticed a familiar figure coming out of Grounds for Celebration, the coffee shop on the corner.

Mayor Beaulieu. Looking smug and untroubled, as usual, carrying a coffee and a bag of doughnuts back across the street to the town hall.

Suddenly he was filled with righteous anger. The mayor had shown nothing but indifference during this economic downturn, hadn't she? She'd refused to consider any initiatives that could help alleviate the desperation and maybe keep a couple more shopfronts from showing "For Lease" signs next year. The town council had done nothing either— too many complacent Holloways in those seats.

He made a point of crossing Mayor Beaulieu's path on his way down the street, toward the little apartment he rented over the general store.

The mayor didn't look up. Ben startled her by saying, "Did you even notice The Old Bookshop was up for sale?"

"Excuse me?" She blinked at him.

"Holloway Green is in trouble," Ben said. He became self-conscious, but someone had to say it. "No one's coming to save us—we have to save ourselves."

"Thank you for that insight," the mayor mumbled. "I greatly value the opinions of constituents." She hurried her pace into Town Hall and slammed the heavy doors behind her.

Ben stared after her, only acknowledging to himself then how much Allison O'Brien had gotten to him. Much as he hated to agree with her, she was right; the town needed to pull itself together, and fast. But there had to be a better first step than... some rich New Yorker buying up the life's work of his grandfather and turning it into a convenience mart.

CHAPTER 3

*T*he stress of running the ski area during an economic slump was apparent in every member of the family.

Mom and Dad, as the manager of the restaurant and pub and the general manager of Jackpine Mountain, respectively, had been in and out of the house frequently last night. They greeted Allison with warmth but only half-attention, and later that night she heard them snapping at each other in the next room.

Her brother Sam, the youngest of the O'Brien siblings, had proved elusive to pin down so far. By the time Allison arrived last night, Sam was out cold after a long day of his duties as operations manager. Today he'd had another long shift—the family was trying to give the non-O'Brien employees a lightened load over Chrismastime—but promised to join them for dinner at Desjardins' Diner.

Christine had been busy today, too, but Allison got the chance to audit a ski class Christine was teaching in the afternoon (skiing and snowboarding lessons were a significant part of Jackpine Mountain's income). Allison had quickly learned how rusty her skills on the slope had gotten, but her sister showed her mercy in front of the other students.

Allison and Christine rode in the backseat of their parents' station wagon over to the diner. Sitting back there made Allison think of when they were younger, picking on each other and trading gross stories, occasionally joining forces to torment their baby brother.

"Sam said he wouldn't be bringing his new girlfriend to dinner," Mom said as she held the door open to the diner for the rest of them. "I told him he could do whatever he wanted, but I was kind of relieved—does that make me a bad person?"

"No, I'd rather keep the drama to a minimum," Dad replied. He still seemed edgy this evening, but Allison hoped a dish of his favorite meatloaf and mashed potatoes would put him in a better mood.

The interior of the diner was much the same as it'd always been, full of kitsch art and decorations that hearkened back to the fifties and sixties, though now adorned with cheap garlands and tinsel, not to mention two terrifying Santa figures—would *effigies* be a more appropriate word?—dangling from the ceiling above the front counter.

As she slid into the booth beside her sister, Allison's thoughts flitted back to Ben and Grandpa Skip at The Old Bookshop. She smiled ruefully, thinking of the handsome, stubble-jawed man rising to his grandfather's defense against her, the oh-so-intrusive prodigal daughter of Holloway Green.

Ben's teenage athleticism had hardened into a leaner strength as an adult, and some of the old warmth had gone from his blunt, coffee-colored gaze. But he was still so good-looking after all these years—scratch that, even *more* good-looking, with the seasoning of maturity—that she'd had to exercise supreme self-control to focus her attention on Grandpa Skip instead of him. Good lord, how embarrassing would it have been if she started stammering and blushing around Ben again… as if she were an awkward girl back in high school again. As if nothing had changed in all those years.

"What are you thinking about, Allie?" Christine asked. "You have a faraway look."

"Aw, nothing," she said.

"C'mon, tell me." Her sister put on a devilish look. "Not Ben Whitfield, is it?"

Allison blushed at being caught out. "No! Goodness, no. Why would—no, I was thinking about all the empty storefronts in Holloway Green. I couldn't really see it last night, but in the daylight, it was obvious how much this town is struggling."

"Any ideas to fix it?"

She shrugged. "I help authors to make their books more readable. And do coffee runs for my jerk of a boss and his friends. Economic redevelopment, that's way out of my area of expertise." She absently played with the glass salt and pepper shakers on the tabletop. "Although… it seems obvious that for a tourist town like Holloway Green, there needs to be things for tourists to actually come *see*. Every loss of an iconic business like The Old Bookshop means one less reason for outsiders to visit." She drew the bowl full of sugar packets closer to her. "So, you…"

Her words faded out as she realized that her sister was looking intently at the salt and pepper shakers in her hands. "What? What is it?"

"Oh, sorry," Christine said. "I thought you were doing one of those 'Let's visualize our master plan to save the town on the table surface with these handy condiments' things."

Allison quirked a smile at her. "Do you *want* me to use the condiments to visualize a master plan to save the town?"

"Only if you feel like it."

"I don't. I don't have a master plan, either! Just saying that if all the places like The Old Bookshop get replaced by generic chain stores and restaurants, then what would be the point of people making a special trip to visit? Jackpine Mountain is a small ski area compared to, like, Pats Peak or one of the conglomerate-owned resorts. People come to our ski area not just because they enjoy our particular slopes and trails, but because they also like shopping and dining in Holloway Green. The mountain and the town are symbiotic. I don't think either could thrive if the other one dies out."

"What's all this talk of dying out?" Dad put in. "Jackpine is doing just fine. And so is Holloway Green, it's just going through a rough patch."

It's not worth fighting with him, not here over dinner. She instead gave their parents a grin and changed the topic. "Are you guys still getting the same things you always get here?"

"You bet," said Dad. "Why would I waste my time with anything but my sweet barbecue meatloaf?"

But Mom smiled back and said, "*I've* branched out. To the Asian chicken dumplings. Darleen has been expanding her culinary powers since you've been gone. I shared a trick or two with her—though not *too* much, since I wouldn't want her to give the Jackpine restaurant any serious competition. I would recommend positively anything on this menu."

Christine leaned in and stage-whispered, "Except for the chicken cacciatore."

Mom gave her a disapproving head-shake. "That was *one time,* and hardly Darleen's fault."

"Don't tell me you ordered without me," someone announced in a loud voice.

"Keep your voice down," Dad said, annoyed.

"Meeerrry Christmas, everyone!" Sam replied, even louder than before, projecting through the entire diner. Heads turned to watch Allison's younger brother stride through the diner, some of the female onlookers appreciating what they saw. But most folks were rolling their eyes.

Sam's cheeks were red from the cold, and he wore a big woolen hat patterned with reindeer. He was twenty-five, gifted with boyish good looks and the same brilliant blue eyes as his sisters, but with a more tenuous grasp on the maturity that ran in the rest of the family. Still, Allison was impressed with how hard he had been working at the ski area—he was definitely growing up.

He squeezed into the booth beside Allison and put his hat on her head. "Hey sis, I'm so glad you could make it home this year," he said.

"Me too," she replied. "But you can have this smelly thing back…"

"How's the powder?" Christine asked.

"Still in good shape," he said. "I don't want to touch a rake for a while again, though." He turned his attention back to Allison. "I can't wait for you to meet Sabrina. You're gonna love her, Allie."

Sam had gone through so many girlfriends since he hit puberty that Allison no longer believed that any of them was going to stick around. He almost always got bored, or did something to sabotage the relationship. But she made an effort to be polite. "Sabrina, that's a nice name."

"She's a dummy," Christine said.

"That's not nice," Mom said immediately.

Christine sighed. "I'm sorry. But—she's got him back into all this stupid spirit world stuff."

"It's not stupid," Sam said, craning his neck past Allison to glare at Christine. "And neither is she. Sabrina is a free

29

thinker in a world full of conformists. That's what I like so much about her."

"Oh," Christine retorted, "not her perfect skin and her pouting lips and—"

"Hey! You've got a lot of nerve criticizing *me* about my love life. Maybe when you jump back in the dating pool one of these decades, you can talk."

Spirit world? Allison shifted her body forward to block her siblings from sniping at each other. She asked her sister, "What do you..." Then she lost her train of thought and sat up straighter as she noticed a familiar blonde figure across the room, serving a table. "Wait, that's... Evie's here working over the holidays?"

"Here working all the time," Dad said. "Things with Ryan, hemm... didn't work out. She moved back here a couple years ago with her kids. I'm surprised you didn't know that."

Allison and Evie Desjardins used to be best friends. They were inseparable as kids. The two had complemented each other: Allison was the shy intellectual, while Evie was outspoken and athletic. They'd kept in touch all throughout college, even though Allison was going to school in Boston and Evie was way out in Chicago. Then... after college graduation, as their career paths diverted, they'd gotten worse at keeping in touch. Or, rather, Allison had, she recalled with guilt. Evie eventually gave up. Allison had known that Evie married a man named Ryan and they had a kid, but...

"How many kids?" she asked.

"Just the two," Mom said.

Just the two. Allison felt another pang of remorse. Quickly followed by dread at what would happen once Evie turned around and noticed her, the neglectful former friend.

"Why don't you say hi when she gets a break?" her sister suggested.

Allison bit her lip. "I... don't know if Evie would want that."

"What'd you do, tell her husband to divorce her?"

"No—I never even got to meet him," she said.

Evie turned. It was too late to flee; Allison was hemmed in by her siblings in the booth. Her old friend caught sight of her and froze. Then, to Allison's immense gratitude, Evie broke into a friendly smile and waved, then tapped her wrist in a gesture that said, *Hang on one minute.* She was either glad to see Allison or doing a masterful job of faking it.

"Evie's been taking on more responsibility here, helping out her mom ever since her dad hurt his back," Mom said. "One of these days Evie might even graduate to co-owner, who knows?"

"She went back to her maiden name," Christine said, "so they won't even have to change the name of the diner."

Their server came over, an older woman with a reindeer antler headband. "Does everyone know what they'd like?"

"Not yet," Sam said, scanning the menu. "Can you come back in ten minutes?"

"Ten minutes?!" Allison gave him a fond jab in the ribs. "Come on, Sam, don't make it into a production."

"Patience," he said. "I make my food choices carefully to avoid a lifetime of regret. For example, what if I foolishly chose the 'breakfast for dinner' special and then got an itching for corned beef later on, an option I hadn't even thought of? I have to peer deep into my soul and ask: *Is the desire for corned beef there?*"

"I don't think I've ever asked myself that," Allison said. "Nor has any other sane human being."

"This is why you're incapable of getting serious with a girl," Christine jabbed at her brother. "You're always afraid there's someone better around the corner. Seize the day, Sam. Get breakfast for dinner. You only live once."

He tsked at her. "If you actually use the acronym 'YOLO,' I'll have to disown you. And you should know, Sabrina and I are *very* serious."

"Right." Christine turned to the server, who was fidgeting with her felt antlers. "We don't have all night. He'll have breakfast for dinner."

The rest of the family placed their orders. Allison thought the new salads on the menu sounded pretty good. Finally, after their server had brought their drinks over, Evie Desjardins came over, looking a little harried.

"Mind if I shimmy in beside you for a moment?" she asked Allison's parents.

Mom smiled. "Of course, dear. Allie was just talking about how excited she was to see you here."

That wasn't quite what Allison had said, of course, but Evie took Mom's words at face value. She leaned across the booth and grasped Allison's hands in hers. "Oh my gosh, I'm excited to see you too, hon. It's been too long. *Way* too long. How's New York treating you?"

I've been stuck in the same position for years, and my boyfriend was cheating on me behind my back... New York really is the city that makes dreams come true!

"It's been great," she said. "I've met a couple of my favorite authors through my publishing job. And I get to think about books all day long... what's not to love?"

Evie's generous mouth broke into a glittering smile. "You've always been so talented, Allie. You deserve all the success you've achieved and more. Listen, I can't linger—Mom's on a holiday-induced warpath—but could we catch up sometime soon? I'm off duty tomorrow."

Allison almost felt like crying, the surge of emotion catching her off guard. Surely she couldn't be so desperate for a taste of simple kindness and friendship... she had those things available already back in the City. Didn't she?

When Peter dumped me, who could I really commiserate with?

"I'm available tomorrow," she said.

"My kids and I are going to pick out a Christmas tree from Lawson's Farm Lot in the afternoon... would you like to help us out?" Without waiting for an answer, Evie scribbled on a napkin and handed it over. "That's my phone. Text me. See you soon, Allie!"

And she hurried off.

"Wonderful," Mom said. "What a wonderful opportunity to reconnect."

But trepidation crept over Allison. It wouldn't be a true connection unless she and Evie were able to open up to each other. And if she couldn't be honest with her own family about the heartache she'd experienced in the City, how could she expect to do so with someone she hadn't talked with in years?

"Hope I didn't just wreck any plans for tomorrow," she said, trying to cover her agitation.

"Plans are fluid," Christine said, "but I'd *love* if you can join me and Dell for some ice skating the day after."

Dell was Christine's longtime friend... emphasis on the *long time,* like since kindergarten. He was an extremely sharp guy who developed websites for nonprofits and had a wicked sense of humor. He had never asked Christine out, but it was clear to Allison, anyway, that he worshiped her. Now that the traumatic Jasper chapter of Christine's life was ancient history, had Dell finally made a move?

"So," Allison said, "are you guys—"

"No," Christine said quickly. "We're just friends."

"I was going to ask if you guys were bringing your own skates."

"Oh." Christine's dark eyebrows drew down. "Sure you were. They have rentals." Then she added crossly, "Dell has been a rock for me during rough times—so I'd *appreciate it* if you don't make any kind of jokes about him, or the two of us. Please."

"I'm sorry, that wasn't my intention," she said. She put a hand on Christine's wrist. "I'm sorry."

"It's okay," Christine said. "Just... don't act like you know everything that's been going on in Holloway Green. Because you don't, all right? You're away most of the time, and... you just don't."

A short silence ensued until their food arrived. Then the O'Briens tucked into their meals with gusto, and the mood brightened. Allison nudged her brother, who had almost half a pancake dangling from his fork. "What's this about the 'spirit world,' Sam? Tell me you aren't getting obsessed with ghosts again."

"O skeptical sis of mine," he said through a mouthful of food, nearly spraying her with crumbs on the consonants, "it's not an obsession. It's a rational inquiry into life after death. The truth behind unexplained phenomena."

"He spent actual money on this nonsense equipment," Christine said. "Just to impress his girlfriend."

"It's only an electromagnetic field meter and a thermographic camera. Well... and night-vision goggles. How much do *you* spend just on clothes each month?"

Christine let out a little bark of indignation. "Clothes! You know I just go to the vintage store most of the time. And clothes actually serve a purpose."

"I'm sorry," Allison broke in, "I didn't mean to start a fight."

Sam gave her a dignified smile. "It's all right. I'm used to suffering slings and arrows from the ignorant. What Chris isn't telling you is that my equipment serves a purpose too. It's already paid for itself."

"Really?"

"Yep!" he said, with obvious pride. "The good folks at the

Carroll County Courthouse in Ossipee hired me earlier this year to investigate something strange they picked up on their security cameras. It was this weird figure that seemed to be moving through walls…"

As she listened to her brother's tale, and the occasional lighthearted jabs her sister put in, Allison found herself hit with a wave of longing—not specific enough that she could truly get her head around it, but still so powerful that it made her draw a shuddering breath. Being here with all her family, sharing stories and teasing each other and enjoying the homey cuisine whipped up by Darleen Desjardins… it all just felt *right* in a way that life in New York hadn't felt for a long time.

Nostalgia's a powerful drug, she tried to remind herself. *Don't romanticize your own hometown.* She knew life was no picnic for her parents or her siblings; they all worked so hard to keep Jackpine Mountain going.

But even if nostalgia were clouding her perceptions right now, she still thought there was truth to her longing underneath. The way she'd felt when her old friend did something as simple as inviting her to hang out, meet her kids, and catch up… something had definitely been missing back in the City, even during the good moments at her job, even before Peter revealed himself to be a slimeball.

When they finished their meal, Darleen Desjardins herself came over and tempted them with the holiday dessert special: a bûche de noel or "Yule log," one of the culinary traditions brought to New Hampshire by French-Canadian immigrants. Everyone protested that they were full, but Sam ordered a piece of the rich, chocolate-frosted and chocolate-filled cake to go.

Back at the house, as Christine was trying to pick out the right schmaltzy holiday movie for the family to watch, Sam said, "Hey, Allie, got a minute?"

"Sure." She went with her brother to the kitchen and flipped on the small overhead light over the breakfast table. Sam put his slice of Yule log in the fridge and then opened a tin on the kitchen counter. He grabbed two cookies shaped like angels from the tin and offered her one, but she declined.

"I heard you saw Ben Whitfield today," he said between bites of his first angel.

She'd hoped to avoid thinking about Ben anymore tonight. She held back a sigh of frustration. "Yeah?"

Sam pursed his lips. "So, Ben and I hang out sometimes. He's helped a lot of people rebuild their homes through that Habitat organization. And you know he's been helping his grandpa fix up the bookstore for free, to prepare for the sale." He paused. "He's... also been pretty lonely ever since he moved back to Holloway Green."

She tensed. Had Sam figured out that she and Peter had broken up? Or was he going to recommend that she dump Peter for Ben Whitfield? Either way, this was awkward. She took a deep breath. "Look, Ben's a great guy..."

"He definitely is," Sam said. "So, I was wondering—would you put in a good word for him when you meet up with Evie Desjardins tomorrow?"

She cocked her head, confused. "A good word for... what? His handyman skills?"

Sam tore into the second angel cookie. "I think they'd make a cute couple. But they both have their shields up. They could use a trusted go-between to get things rolling..."

Oh.

Allison's mouth dropped open. It was funny, really, that Sam wanted to fix those two up... wasn't it? *No, it's not funny. Ben and Evie really would make a cute couple.*

So why do I feel sick to my stomach about it?

"Are you sure they'd... make a good match?" she asked, stumbling over her words. "I mean, Ben's—he's kind of hard to read. He was even a little rude to me when I stopped into the bookstore. Like, almost like he resented my offer to help Grandpa Skip."

"I'm sure you misinterpreted that," Sam said. Now *he* was sounding defensive. Allison had no idea they'd grown to be such close friends, her brother and her...

Old crush.

No, her random schoolmate from days long past.

"You're right," she said. "I'm sure it was awkwardness, since we hadn't seen each other in a long time. It's just... Evie's a very nice girl, and—she has two young kids. What if Ben took off from Holloway Green again someday? Didn't he only return to town recently?"

"Two years ago. That's not recent." Sam sounded faintly outraged. "He was helping people build and rebuild houses, communities. He's an exemplary guy. Are you saying he can't be trusted?"

"No. But as Mom said, Evie's been through a lot, and she's stepping up her responsibilities at the diner. I don't want someone to waste her time."

"He wouldn't."

"What's your stake in this, anyway?" she asked. "You've never tried to play matchmaker with anyone before."

He shrugged. "Want to help a friend, is all. And... Ben doesn't seem to want to hang out so much lately, ever since I started dating Sabrina. I think he might be a touch jealous of my relationship. But if he's got his own ladyfriend, we could double date."

That all sounded unlikely to Allison, especially the part about Ben Whitfield being jealous of Sam for anything. But of course, she'd been gone from Holloway Green for a while, and who knew how much the social dynamics had changed. "I guess...?"

"Just remember to give Ben some good press when you're

talking to Evie. Thanks so much for your help, sis, you're a sweetheart."

And he kissed her on the cheek, placed a candy cane-shaped cookie in front of her, as if it were an offering, and left the kitchen. Allison blew out an annoyed breath. *I didn't really agree to it...*

Partway through the holiday movie, as Dad and Christine were both nodding off on opposite ends of the big blue couch, Allison's phone jangled. Dad snorted, looking around with bleary eyes. "Is that… who's that…"

"Sorry, Dad!" She hopped up to take the call in a different room. "Hello?"

"Little pretzel? Can you hear me?"

The gravelly voice belonged to one of the booksellers she'd contacted earlier today, a prime weirdo named Valentino Boggs. He was a bibliophile and a businessman with loads of money attached to his name, and not from selling books.

"I can, yes, Mr. Boggs," she said. "Thanks for calling me b—"

"I'm *highly* interested in this Old Bookshop you speak of," he said. "It sounds like a rare prize, as does the community surrounding it. I had my assistant brief me on the history, culture, and economy of Holloway Green, and I sense a region ripe for prosperity. Thus I had that same assistant book me a flight to New England to check out the shop for myself."

"Oh," she said surprised. "A flight?" She hadn't expected things to move *this* quickly. "When are you, um, planning to grace The Old Bookshop with your presence, Mr. Boggs?"

"Tomorrow morning, my pretzel," said Valentino Boggs.

Tomorrow? Tomorrow morning?! Allison stared at the screen of her phone in alarm. It was already past ten. She imagined

Grandpa Skip would already be in bed if she tried to call him. This was a little too fast.

And what was up with this "pretzel" nickname?

"Actually, that might be premature, Mr. Boggs," she said quickly. "The owner isn't one hundred percent certain he's going to sell the bookstore to someone from outside of New England." It had been Ben, not Grandpa Skip, who insisted that the buyer should be local, so she wasn't sure why she was pressing this particular point—really she was just stalling for time.

"Then he'll just need some convincing in person," Boggs said. "I'm arriving at, hmm, Manchester-Boston Regional Airport at eleven. Now, is that in Manchester or is it in Boston?"

"Manchester."

"As I thought. We'll be in touch."

"Wait," she said, but the bookseller had already hung up. Allison didn't want to call him back and risk souring a lucrative deal for Grandpa Skip before it could be given a chance. Boggs, a wealthy man dripping with power and influence, wasn't used to people telling him what he could or couldn't do.

What have I done?

Was Holloway Green even ready for the likes of Valentino Boggs?

CHAPTER 4

a ridiculously large silver car rolled into Holloway Green. Ben turned to watch the car as it passed him and then parked over by the gazebo, in a handicapped spot, though it didn't have the proper plates; it was a rental.

"Get a load of that monster," said Tony, the grizzled, cheerful proprietor of Antonio's Ristorante. He was heading down the sidewalk toward Ben with an enormous plastic bag slung over his shoulder. He shook his shaggy head in disbelief. "We got a movie star coming into town or what?"

"Someone rich, that's for sure," Ben replied. He took a closer look at the bag Tony was carrying. It was stuffed with red fabric and white, furry material. "What do you have in there? Looks like you just kidnapped Santa."

"In a sense," the older man said. He looked embarrassed. "I gotta moonlight as Mr. Claus himself at parties to make a little extra scratch. Business at Antonio's has been… a little slow. Headed over to Mountaintop Winery to put on a show for some corporate types."

"Knock 'em dead," Ben said. He was disappointed to hear that even a great restaurant like Antonio's was struggling right now. As Tony headed off to his Santa gig, an unpleasant thought occurred to Ben, and he looked back toward the silver car.

Oh no. Don't tell me this is one of Allison's "prospective buyers."

The man who unfolded from the silver car was huge, massive even: a bald bruiser in a white suit and black shirt and tie. He looked like a mafia boss, not a candidate for owning a small-town bookstore. He carried himself with more grace than Ben expected from his bulk, striding over to a nearby woman whom he towered over. The bald man leaned down and planted a rather formal kiss on each of her cheeks. European, perhaps?

Ben noticed then who the woman was: Allison.

"Hoo boy," he muttered. He hated being right.

Allison and the gigantic stranger began a conversation that Ben couldn't hear at this distance. He ran to the bookstore and locked the door behind him, then put his back against it. Grandpa Skip wasn't here; he'd told Ben earlier that he had to work on a "project," and refused to elaborate. Maybe Grandpa Skip's project was simply avoiding this prospective buyer.

If that was the case, Ben could hardly blame his grandfather. When Allison had been talking about New York buyers yesterday, the idea had seemed remote, abstract. But one of them actually showing up in person—the very next day!—gave Ben heartburn. The thought of losing The Old Bookshop from the family now felt horribly real.

We'll just see about that.

He unlocked the door again and then stepped away before Allison and her guest could think he was barring them from entering. Not that a physical contest between himself and the bald man would end in anything but tears; Ben was a big man, but the man in the white suit had to be almost seven feet tall and over three hundred pounds. Ben picked up a hammer and went to a nearby bookcase where he'd been replacing one of the shelves, posing as if he'd been occupied this whole time.

What is Allison thinking, springing this guy on me without warning? This was a game to her, a power trip. People from New York thought the world revolved around them. *Good thing I can play the game right back...*

He heard them talking as they approached the bookstore. "...been hard on everyone," Allison was saying. "That's one of the reasons The Old Bookshop ran into trouble in the first place. The town depends on tourism dollars, and when those dry up because tourists are reducing their spending, it has a cascading effect."

"Still, it's charming," the bald man said, his voice husky, as Allison held the door open for him and he ducked inside. Funny, he didn't have a European accent. The cheek kisses must have been an affectation. He was holding a big, steaming cup of coffee from Grounds for Celebration.

Ben pretended to be surprised to see them. He raised his hammer in a salute. "Oh hello," he said. "Sorry this place is a mess, I was just finishing up some—"

"Oh hello yourself," the stranger said, his feet thudding on the wooden floor, sending vibrations Ben could feel through his boots. The man offered a huge hand. "My name is Valentino Boggs, and I'm going to purchase your bookstore."

The New Yorker's arrogance angered him. He forced himself to respond calmly: "Is that so? I'm sorry, but I don't think I know you."

"You will soon enough," this Valentino Boggs said, "and the experience will be *transformative*. For both of us." He flashed Ben a smile that surely wasn't intended to look as predatory as it did.

Help. Ben shot a look at Allison, who said, "Mr. Boggs,

this is Ben, the owner's grandson. Ben, is Grandpa Skip here?"

"No," Ben said. "I'm sorry, but he's not sure about selling the place yet."

"That's not what he was saying yesterday," Allison said sharply.

Boggs spread his huge arms and said, "I'm sure you can track down the grandfather so I can talk to him myself, Alice. Ben, I'd like to take a look around the bookstore regardless."

Ben swept his arm toward the white-suited man in an ironic flourish. "Be my guest."

"I am," Boggs said. He proceeded in a circuit around the store, poking his nose in every section. Ben tensed as the huge man mounted the stairs to the loft level, suddenly picturing the worst, and considered warning him about the shakiness of the railing. But the New Yorker seemed sure of his footing, reaching the top with no greater consequence than constantly rattling shelves throughout the store. He grunted to himself as he inspected the shelves and the inventory.

Ben pretended not to care, working on a small repair. Allison leafed through a book; her cheeks seemed red. When Boggs returned to them, he was grinning, a frightening sight indeed.

"This place has excellent bones," Boggs rumbled. "Hardly any part of it will have to be significantly gutted. I could see a coffee shop right over *here*, a reading nook and performance space over *there*, and—"

"There's a coffee shop right across the street," Ben said, alarmed. "I assume you noticed, since you're holding one of their coffees. See, I don't think Grandpa Skip would want the bookstore to compete with their business."

"When I operate this bookstore," Boggs said, folding his

arms, "you won't need to be concerned about the coffee shop across the street. It will no longer be a problem."

Maybe he really is in the mafia. "What's that supposed to mean?"

"It doesn't mean anything," Allison interjected. Ben turned to her in annoyance. "Mr. Boggs is just thinking out loud. He hasn't had time to get to know the community yet. I'm sure that nothing significant about the bookstore would change under Mr. Boggs's ownership."

"Sure," Ben said. "Nothing significant is going to change. Because Grandpa Skip shouldn't sell The Old Bookshop to an outsider. You know what? Maybe I'll buy the bookstore and operate it myself."

Valentino Boggs's brow furrowed as he turned his attention to Allison. "You didn't tell me the owner was considering that as a possibility."

"I didn't know this possibility was … a possibility," Allison said, looking confused.

Ben was bluffing, but he enjoyed seeing her squirm. He put down the hammer and gave her a direct stare—*Do you think I'm joking?*—until he found himself falling into those deep blue eyes and had to look away.

"Did this person work at the bookstore previously?" Boggs asked her. Apparently he'd had enough of speaking to Ben directly.

"I have," Ben butted in. "I've helped Grandpa Skip out plenty of times. And I've been reading plenty of books on managing small businesses. Whatever I don't know yet, I can learn, and fast."

"I suppose my business here is done before it begins, then," Boggs said, making his voice boom even louder than usual. Both Allison and Ben jumped. The huge man made a dramatic turn toward the door.

"Wait," Allison said. "This isn't *Ben's* decision to make. It's his grandfather's. Mr. Boggs, you need to connect with Grandpa—with Skip Whitfield himself. As you said, I'll track him down. Will you be staying in town?"

"Yes," the man replied stiffly, "but not for long. I do have my own family to return to for Christmas."

"Great," Allison said. "I'll arrange a meeting for you with Mr. Whitfield as soon as possible."

"Keep me posted, I want to be at that meeting," Ben said.

"I look forward to it," Boggs said dryly. "If you'll both excuse me, I must check in at the bed and breakfast where I'm staying."

Allison reached up to touch his elbow. "Do you want me to help you find it? I can take you there."

He strode away from her. "No need." And he ducked under the doorframe on his way out.

Allison, when she turned to Ben, was radiant with fury. Her blue eyes had gone from enchanting to penetrating, as if they could bore right through him. "What are you doing?" she demanded.

"Keeping the wrong person from taking over Grandpa Skip's legacy," he said. "I *do* want to run the bookstore. I've wanted that for a long time."

That was technically true, but he hadn't seriously thought about *buying* the bookstore himself until this very moment—he had always pictured it as more of a partnership with his grandfather, or acting as Grandpa Skip's general manager. But… was buying the place such a crazy thought? He had some money socked away, and he could borrow more.

No, that is *crazy.*

"It's not your decision to make," Allison said. "Have you even talked to your grandfather about this?"

"Sort of."

"Oh yeah? You could've mentioned that possibility to me

when I was offering to help," she said. "Before I went through all the trouble of connecting with buyers."

"I never told you to do that," Ben said, annoyed.

She looked like she wanted to smack him across the face. She didn't. "Are you sure you don't know where Grandpa Skip is? I left him a voicemail last night that a potential buyer would be in town, but it was late, and I never heard back from him. I'll call him again."

"No, I'll do it," he said. "It's our family business. Not your business."

He hadn't meant it as a final insult. But clearly Allison took it that way.

"I'm sure Boggs could offer your grandfather a lot more money for the bookstore than you could," she said. "Unless you unearthed a chest full of doubloons or something during your aid missions. Like I said, it's Grandpa Skip's choice—don't rob him of it. Now I've got to go meet a friend."

And she left.

Ben fumed for a little while after she was gone, which made further repairs to the bookstore difficult without injuring himself.

Slowly, however, the bluff he'd made to Allison came to resemble something else in his mind: a challenge. A rebuke to the callous stranger that she'd brought into the store, this wealthy, hulking dilettante who thought he could snap his fingers and remake a crucial piece of Holloway Green into his own twisted, big-city image.

Grandpa Skip genuinely loved not only books, but creating a place where the whole community could feel comfortable, could learn and be entertained and connect with each other. Would that all still happen when a stranger took over the property? Ben thought it'd be highly unlikely in the hands of someone like Valentino Boggs.

The buyer should be someone Grandpa Skip knows. Someone he can trust. Someone local.

Ben had been preparing for the day that Grandpa Skip gave him a chance with the bookstore, if it ever arrived. He'd read everything he could find about operating small businesses, borrowing books on the subject from the store itself (and carefully returning them in perfect condition). He'd been operating on the assumption that Grandpa Skip would still be involved in the bookstore too, but... Ben was thirty-four years old. If he couldn't learn to handle helming the ship solo by now, he never could.

He locked up the shop and left.

Grandiose thoughts kept deviling him. The cold of the afternoon seemed to slough away. *I can't believe you're considering this. You not only don't have the know-how, you don't have the money.*

Well, he had some... but not enough. But that was what business loans were for.

If Grandpa Skip could get a big payout from a rich New Yorker like Valentino Boggs, Ben knew he shouldn't be standing in the way. Grandpa Skip could sure use the extra money; he deserved the money. But Ben could still give his grandfather a fair price for the shop, and wouldn't it be worth the slightly smaller payout if the old man knew he could trust the owner to keep his life's work intact?

You're crazy.

The idea wouldn't go away. He found himself walking faster, loosening his scarf while he collected a fragmented plan in his head. He would have to learn much more than he already knew about the business, but he had the discipline and the determination to do so. Grandpa Skip could teach him plenty, but Ben could also get up to speed on new ideas and techniques for running a small business like a bookstore that his grandfather might not know about. Grandpa Skip had resisted innovation, but innovation didn't mean giving up the soul of the shop.

Yes.

I'm going to bring The Old Bookshop back to life and run it myself.

His breath pluming, the snow sparkling all around him, Ben Whitfield headed to his apartment above the general store to make a plan.

CHAPTER 5

*A*llison smiled broadly as Evie's two kids came running to greet her in the parking area of the Christmas tree lot, their mother trying to catch up. The daughter, Frannie, reached Allison first. "Hi Miss O'Brien! Mommy says you're an expert tree picker!"

She laughed. "I think your mommy might have exaggerated a little bit. It's nice to meet you, Frannie. And you've got to be Nicky, right?"

"Hi hi," said the younger child, a boy with hair sticking out wildly from around his earmuffs. He was definitely shyer than his sister; his courage broke and he ran to hide behind Evie's legs as Allison approached.

"Good morning," said Evie. "Thanks again for joining us, Allie... they've been so excited to meet you."

Me? Why? she wondered. *Because kids are just great that way, I guess.* Allison grinned and handed Evie a steaming coffee cup from Grounds for Celebration. "My treat. I hope you like a little milk and sugar."

"That's perfect," Evie said cheerily. "Thanks!" She looked

down at her kids. "See how nice Miss O'Brien is? She's going to help us find the most Christmasy tree in the lot."

"That's a lot of pressure," Allison remarked. "I'll do my very best, though!"

The four of them headed into the maze of trees offered by Lawson's Farm Lot—mostly balsam firs, but with some of the western export, Douglas firs, available as well. If you *really* wanted a tree that exactly fit your needs, you could make a visit to Lawson's Tree Farm itself and cut one down from their vast holdings. But Evie was perfectly happy with getting one of the pre-cut trees at the lot, which Allison was grateful for. She didn't relish the thought of getting fir sap on her cashmere coat.

As the kids went ahead to scout for trees they liked, Allison said, "I need to apologize to you. I should have done a *much* better job keeping in touch over the years. I just got... lost in the swirl of activity in my job, the excitement in the City, and I—well, I'd still think about you, Evie, but I never quite got around to connecting with you. Even when you reached out, I somehow didn't find the energy to reply most of the time... I don't know why. Something defective in me, I guess."

"I forgive you," Evie said simply.

"Really?"

"Really," Evie repeated, breaking into a warm smile. "Now we can move past all that and be friends again. How does that sound?"

Allison stopped and stared at her. "I—I'd love that, but how can you just forgive me for treating you like dirt? Like our friendship had meant nothing? I don't know if I'd be able to forgive *me*, if I were in your position."

"You would," Evie said quietly. "Because... if you were in my position, you would have been through the 'miracle' of motherhood twice and a messy divorce, and would thus have the wisdom to realize that life's too short to hold grudges. Life is meant for embracing other people. If someone comes back into your life, don't take that for granted."

Allison's eyes stung. She pretended to inspect the nearest tree, a gnarly little specimen with a bald patch the size of a diner pancake. "Thank you," she said. "That means a lot."

It struck her how Evie had grown up from a chatty, impulsive teenager to a mature adult, someone seasoned but not broken by difficult times. And Allison had missed out on Evie's transformation completely. *How much do I even know her now?* She was determined to find out.

"Now, I want to hear everything," Evie said. "All about your New York adventures, and those favorite authors you actually got the chance to meet. Don't leave out the painful stuff, either. I'm here for it all."

"Well, wait," Allison said. "Before I get my big mouth going, I want to know about you. How long have you been living back in Holloway Green?"

"Almost two years," Evie said. "After Ryan and I ended up with… irreconcilable differences, I decided I wanted the kids to be closer to their grandparents. Also—it's quite possible I'd had enough of bland, cookie-cutter suburban life."

She flashed a quick smile full of white, even teeth. Evie was even prettier than she'd been in high school and college. She had grown into her truer self. An unwelcome note of jealousy followed, as Allison briefly pictured Ben Whitfield and Evie holding hands, walking toward a gazebo or something… they would make a *very* good-looking couple.

I don't have to say anything. I could tell Sam to stuff it.

But why *not* set them up? It wasn't like Ben would get together with Allison. He clearly wanted nothing to do with her, after their fight at The Old Bookshop (which she'd capped off with a petty insult of his financial status). And she would just be heading back to New York after the holidays anyway. Jealousy was… irrational.

"Our h-hometown does have a lot of character," Allison said, stumbling over her words, as she attempted to banish the image of a paired-up Ben and Evie from her mind. "I'm sure your parents were glad to have you living back in town."

Evie nodded, but hesitantly. "Yeah… for the most part. I mean, yeah. Dad was. My mom too. But Mom had, uh, always been hoping that Ryan would move back here with me. She had a hard time understanding how I could let such a prize of a man go."

Allison flinched from the bitterness that had entered her old friend's voice. She let out a little cloud of frosted breath. "Oh, I'm… sorry. That must have been difficult for you."

Evie nodded. "Yeah. I mean, Mom's come around since then—mostly. But she can't wrap her mind around two people just falling out of love. She's still so intensely in love with Dad even after all these years, these decades. She thinks a failed marriage, or any kind of relationship, always has to be *someone*'s fault, and since she always saw Ryan as this perfect guy…"

"It had to be your fault," Allison finished for her. That *was* hard.

And relatable.

You're afraid of what Dad will say. Isn't that the real reason you haven't told the family that Peter cheated on you and dumped you? You think Dad will take Peter's side, even without having ever met him…

No. That couldn't be true. And yet… Dad had always had exacting standards for his children to live up to. He believed in personal responsibility, in taking the blame for any failure, and he'd drilled that mentality into all of them. Even Sam had risen to meet Dad's expectations over the years; just look at how hard he was working at the ski area.

She remembered the awful week when Christine's fiancé, Jasper, had broken off their engagement. Christine had been more than upset; she'd felt broken herself. And Dad had been a big part of that. *What did you do to make him leave you, Christine? There must have been* something. *Are you sure there wasn't* something, *girl?*

Allison shivered, hit by a wave of empathy and pity for her younger sister all over again. Dad had apologized soon after, calling it a temporary fit of insanity, but… had Christine ever forgotten?

"You've been through a lot," Allison said, forcing her attention back to Evie's story. "But your kids seem very happy and sweet. You've done a great job with them."

"Aw, thank you," her old friend said. "They're great kids to begin with, I just try not to mess them up."

Allison still felt like she was missing pieces about who Evie was now, beyond her kids and the divorce. She reached back to details from school, testing them out. "Do you still play any soccer, like, in a rec league?"

"Oh, I'm too afraid of pulling something now," Evie said, smiling. "But Frannie's on a team. I can live vicariously through her. If you're asking about hobbies, I've taken an interest in history the past few years. Do some volunteering at the historical society. I could bore you with some stories."

"I'd like that," Allison said.

Frannie and Nicky galloped back to them. "Mom! Miss O'Brien! We found a good one. Come on."

Allison inspected the tree. "This one *is* nice, guys. But see that patch of brown branches right there? I bet we could do even better."

"I'll find the best one first!" Nicky squealed, and charged off. His sister went after him, calling for him to wait up already.

"Now this one's kind of nice," Allison said, moving on to

another tree. She perfunctorily inspected the branches, but her mind was on the thing—the man—she would have to talk about sooner or later.

Evie, looking at the same fir, missed Allison's nervousness. She said, "I'd like one a tiny bit taller, I think. But not so tall it scrapes the living room ceiling!" Then she glanced at Allison, her hazel eyes twinkling. "So, your turn! I want to hear about the big city, the excitement, the magic—tell me everything."

Magic. Hmm. "I'll try to boil it down to my greatest hits," she said.

She told Evie about her entrance into the promising world of publishing, advancement for a while, and then hitting a wall, where she'd lingered for a few years now. Her first apartment, with its, well, rodent problem, and the series of her "unforgettable" (in both the good and bad senses) roommates in the City. Her adventures in dating, including... Peter.

She was surprised to find herself talking openly about the breakup. His admission that he'd been cheating on her for months. The block that she'd felt preventing her from telling the truth to her family—it had cleared as she reknit the bond of her friendship with Evie.

When she finished, she looked around, blinking, as the world of New York faded and was replaced by the tree lot. "Sorry to blab on for so long," she said. "I don't think I've been that open with anyone in... quite some time. Peter included."

"Thank you for sharing all that with me," Evie said. "You've given me a great gift just by talking about *adult stuff* with me... my conversations at home revolve around cartoon characters on TV, or whatever video game Frannie is playing."

"That... must get old!" Allison said. Then she added,

"Evie, do you mind not mentioning anything about Peter to my family? I haven't had the heart to tell them about the breakup yet. They think he was just too busy with work to come up here and meet them."

Evie nodded, but she looked troubled. "You don't feel like you can talk to them about it?"

"I just… I keep not wanting to ruin the limited family time we have together. Especially during the holidays. I don't want to be a downer."

Evie shrugged. "A thought. If you lived around here, you would have all the time in the world to talk to them…" She shook her head abruptly. "I'm overstepping. Sorry. I just know they miss you."

"I miss them too," Allison said thoughtfully.

Then she remembered Sam's painful request. She would prove to herself that she wasn't jealous at all at the thought of Evie and Ben becoming an item. After all, they both deserved to be happy. She cleared her throat.

"I found a potential buyer for The Old Bookshop," Allison said. "From the City. He's here in town now."

"Oh? Which city? Boston?"

Allison chuckled at her own expense. Yes, obviously up here people didn't think of New York as the only City worth mentioning. No one could hear the capital C in her voice. "Sorry, I meant New York. I know a bunch of booksellers back there. The one in town is ready to make an offer for The Old Bookshop."

"That's terrific," Evie said. "I'd love to see that bookstore reopen. And I could see the charm it'd have for someone from a big city. Especially if they've been thinking about escaping to a cute little town anyway. What does Grandpa Skip think?"

"I haven't been able to get a hold of him yet," Allison said. "Ben, his grandson, said he wanted to buy out Grandpa

Skip and take over the place himself, but that's clearly ridiculous."

The afternoon was still and clear, the bright blue sky shining down without a hint of snow. Evie breathed in happily. "Why would it be ridiculous? I'm sure he'd be more than capable."

Allison realized she was already failing to make Ben look good. "Oh, you know what, you're right. He's capable. Quite a good-looking guy too." Then cursed her own ineptitude. Now that last part sounded like it'd come out of nowhere…

Her friend shot her a curious look. "Um… yeah. Also an important quality for running a bookstore, I suppose."

"Gotta keep the lady customers coming back," she said, and forced a laugh. It came out like a hiccup. *Come on, get it together.*

"Are you all right?" Evie asked. "I've got some water if you need it. I always bring a bottle for the kids."

"No, I'm fine," Allison said, reddening. "I… um. I just admire how Ben has been helping Grandpa Skip fix up the bookstore. He's been putting in a lot of time renovating and repairing it for free."

"Well, it's not *really* for free, if he wants to buy the bookstore," said Evie equably.

"I just mean," Allison blurted, "I think he's very generous. And handsome. And… good with a hammer. Don't you?"

Evie furrowed her brow and looked at Allison. "Oh," she said. "You're developing feelings for him, are you? That's sweet! You two would make an excellent couple. You—"

"No, no," Allison said, holding up both arms as if to ward off the notion. "I don't. I mean, he's great. *Really* great. But I don't…"

"You don't have to pretend around me," Evie said. "How long do we go back? I can see it in your face, hear it in your voice. You really like this guy."

Allison balled her fists in frustration. "No. He's stubborn and a little rude. He's not my type at all! But he'd be absolutely perfect for *you*."

Evie stopped walking. Her features hardened, though her voice was level when she spoke. "All right. Stubborn and rude… that's a type that would fit well with me?"

"No," Allison protested. "That's not what I meant. He's big and strong and kindhearted, and *that* would definitely be a great match for you, Evie."

Her friend let out a deep breath, then called her kids back to her. She looked at the array of Christmas trees as if not seeing them, her eyes seeming unfocused. Evie ran a hand through Frannie's hair and spoke to Allison without looking at her. "That's… very nice of you to say, Allison. But I'm—I'm not interested in being the subject of matchmaking. Not now. Maybe not ever. I have a full life already, surely you…"

Evie's voice faded.

Allison, eager to agree with her, said, "Yes. Of course. I totally understand. Please don't take offense, Evie. I didn't mean to be insensitive."

"No, it's fine," Evie said, shaking her head. Finally her eyes met Allison's. "I just feel a little silly, that's all. Honestly misread the situation when you were talking about Ben… I am off my game. Rusty." She let out a little mirthless laugh. "Hey, why don't we dig down into finding that tree?" She looked down at her kids. "Any leads?"

"I found the bestest one," Nicky announced. "Lemme show you!"

"It's not the best," Frannie said.

"Well, we'd better check it out," Allison said. "Lead the way, my friends."

As she followed the little family, she gave her brother a few choice words in her head. Sam's dumb idea had endangered her friendship with Evie, just when they'd finally knitted it together again. Ben Whitfield could do his own stupid matchmaking...

I wonder if he's even looking.

The notion unsettled her thoughts for the rest of the tree-hunting operation. As did the thought that Evie had seen through her after all.

CHAPTER 6

"*Y*ou're a natural," Ben said to the teenage girl trailing behind him. "You've got this, Sarah."

His niece hesitated to step onto the ice, even though she'd already found the courage to strap on her skates. "Maybe… I'll just watch you for a while, Uncle B." (She liked to call him that so he wouldn't sound like "the rice guy.")

Ben shook his head. "That's a no-can-do, my friend. You have to come out at the same time I do. Otherwise I'll just look like a loser, skating all by myself. Can you help me out here?"

That got a smile from Sarah. She nodded shakily, and put a skate blade out on the ice. Two skaters in their twenties in matching blue hats veered wide around Sarah to give her room as they passed.

"There you go. Now the other one."

She stuck her other leg out on the ice too, then started to tumble. She grabbed the rink railing and clung to it. "No, see… I'm not ready."

"You know how to do this," Ben reminded her. "Just

because you fell that one time, doesn't mean you have to fall again. Even if you do, I'll be there to catch you." He offered her a gloved hand. "Come on, now, Sarah. Remember, your uncle has to avoid being a social pariah out on the ice, all by his lonesome."

"That is so dumb," Sarah said with feeling, but she took his hand. Together they joined the circling crowd around the rink.

Grey hung over the afternoon, but so far snow had held off, and it seemed like half of Holloway Green was out on the ice. Each winter, the historical society partnered with the town department of recreation to set up the rink at Bilberry Park. Admission fees went toward operating the historical sites at Bilberry during the warmer months.

True to Ben's expectations, as soon as they got in the rhythm, Sarah forgot her trepidation and started enjoying herself, even outpacing him until their linked hands either forced him to speed up or dragged her back. Ben felt an intense rush of pride for her, getting back on her skates and overcoming her fears. Her bad fall last week had been a freak accident, one she was unlikely to repeat as long as she stayed confident (but not cocky).

Like so much of life, he thought to himself, amused. *Strike a healthy balance between cowardice and cockiness.*

As they rounded the next circuit of the rink, he saw Allison O'Brien with some red-haired guy, skating close together, laughing—and appearing to Share a Moment. And Ben abruptly lost his balance.

"Come on, Uncle B!" Sarah cried out, sounding embarrassed. She managed to pull him up before he spun out. Too late to preserve his dignity, he looked up and saw Allison staring straight at him curiously.

Ugh. He looked over at his niece. "Thanks for saving my butt there. What did I tell you, you're a natural!"

"What just happened?" she asked, scrunching her eyes at him. "Was that a test?"

"Uh… yeah," he said. "You passed. Congrats, kid!"

She chuffed. He tried to look away as Allison and the random red-haired dude circled nearer to them on this go-round. He now realized that there was another person with them: Christine, Allison's younger sister. That made him feel a little better—that they were a trio, not Allison alone with a male townie—but not much. Jealousy wasn't sitting easy with him.

Maybe he's not a townie... maybe this is the mysterious New York boyfriend. Be nice.

So, Ben was nice, all right—when Allison gestured at him to come off the ice and talk, he did acknowledge her. But with a shrug, not an immediate move to obey. Couldn't she see that he was busy mentoring his niece on the ice?

"Who's that?" Sarah said.

"An old classmate," he said, hoping it sounded dismissive.

"She's hot," Sarah said. "If she wants you to get off the rink and talk to her, you definitely should. I'll be fine out here on my own."

"Sarah—"

She let go of his hand and gave him a gentle push away. "Really. You've helped me a ton today, Uncle B. I feel so much more confident."

"Oh—okay," he said. At the next opportunity, he found the exit off the rink and went over to the O'Brien sisters and the red-haired guy. The maybe-boyfriend looked quite a bit dorkier now than he had at first glance, with huge, staring green eyes that matched the pom-pom on his winter hat.

Ben looked back toward Sarah, concerned about her skating by herself despite her claim of confidence… and saw her maneuvering toward a boy in a violet scarf who was around her own age. *Very sneaky*, he thought; he was impressed.

"Hey," Allison said. "Didn't expect to see you out here. Who was your friend?"

"My niece Sarah," he said stiffly. "I didn't expect... well, how are you folks doing?" *Be nice*, he remembered. He extended a hand toward the red-haired man. "You must be the boyfriend. I'm Ben, it's great to meet you."

"The boyfriend?" the guy said, baffled.

Ben became mortified as he recognized who the man was: Dell Gagnon, Christine's good friend. He had run into Dell plenty of times around town before. He just must not have recognized him because of the big goofy hat with the pom-pom. *And because you didn't know what you were seeing... only what you dreaded to see. Jealousy blinded you, Ben.*

His face felt hot. "Forgive me. A misunderstanding."

"He's not my boyfriend," Christine said, looking stormy.

"Not mine either," Allison said, with a chiding look at her sister, "though any girl would be lucky to call Dell Gagnon her boyfriend." She gave Dell a friendly pat on the shoulder and then gazed curiously at Ben. "Not to extend the moment of awkwardness, but... whose boyfriend did you think Dell was, Ben? Mine or Christine's?"

"Never mind," he said, disgusted. "I'm just... you called me off the ice and away from my niece. Is there something you need?"

"Spoken like a man with a hot chocolate deficiency," Dell remarked, in a not unfriendly way.

Christine cuffed him on the arm. "You know what, Dell, that's an excellent idea. We'll get a round of hot cocoa for everyone, including Ben's niece. Allie, we'll be right back."

"Oh, you don't need to..." Allison started, then faded off when she saw she couldn't stop her sister.

"I don't mean to be rude," Ben said, relenting at the

stricken look on Allison's face. "I was only confused because we… didn't leave things on good terms, last we saw each other."

"You could say that," Allison admitted. "I've been unprofessional, Ben, and I apologize—I should have given you a heads up about Valentino Boggs when I couldn't reach your grandfather. I didn't know that you were considering buying the bookstore, either. I was just surprised."

He scratched his chin and said gruffly, "There's no need to apologize. I know you were just trying to help."

"Have you talked with Grandpa Skip about it? Like, how much you could offer him for the bookstore?"

Um… "I'm going to tonight."

"Now, Boggs hasn't made an offer yet," Allison said, lowering her voice. "But he probably will when he meets with Grandpa Skip tomorrow morning."

"Tomorrow morning? Where?" *And why didn't Grandpa Skip tell me?*

"At Grounds for Celebration. I know you wanted to be there, so… be there. Just know that Boggs has deep pockets, and your grandfather could retire very comfortably. Be careful not to put any undue pressure on him to sell to you rather than Boggs, unless you're *absolutely* sure this is what you want to do. Your claim this morning just seemed a little sudden." She inclined her head at him. "I want everyone's best interests to be represented here, so—um—sleep on it, would you?"

That was reasonable enough. "All right."

She leveled a cool gaze at him. "And remember that running an independent bookstore in the twenty-first century is no joke. I've seen it eat people alive back in New York. By the time the really brilliant ideas hit you about how to be profitable, you may have run the store into the ground already. Leaving no book stock left to sell along with the store, because you've already sold it all at a loss just to keep the lights on. And a bookstore without books is… just a building."

He bristled at this assessment of his ability, but then he noticed Christine and Dell returning with the hot chocolates, all five balanced in their grasp. "I'll make it work. Do him proud."

Dell handed him a hot chocolate with an overly broad smile. Ben took the cocoa and took a sip, too quickly. "Ow."

"Careful, it's hot," Dell said, still smiling.

Jerk. Ben gripped the hot chocolate tighter. "But delicious. Thanks for the treat, my friend."

"Anytime."

"I'll take the one for Sarah over to her," Ben said, holding a hand out. Christine gave him one of the ones she was holding. "I guess I'll see you at the meeting tomorrow morning, then, Allison?"

Allison frowned. "Oh. No. It's business, and not mine, so my meddling ends here. Good luck at the meeting, though. Be clear on what you really want before you walk in there."

Christine gave him a sage nod. "I don't know what we're talking about, but I totally agree."

"And can you find out why he keeps calling me 'pretzel'?" Allison added. "I never got the chance to find out."

"Um, of course."

"What?" Dell said, looking from Allison to Ben. Then he gave up and drank from his steaming cup.

Ben went over to the rink railing and waited for Sarah to tire so he could give her the hot chocolate. He remained placid on the surface, but his thoughts were whirling.

BEN DROVE Sarah back to his sister's horse farm. He parked

near the barn and went in to say hello to the horses for a moment. They were beauties. Both Meghan and Sarah loved to ride through the countryside in milder seasons. He stroked Ace's long head and said, "Good boy."

Then he followed Sarah into the farmhouse, which was redolent with the delicious smell of baking bread. Meghan was busy in the kitchen, looking panicked. Unlike Ben, she had gotten most of her good looks from their late mother, with her dusky complexion inherited from Mom's Armenian family. At forty she was even more radiant than she had ever been, though just now her features were creased into a puzzled look.

"Give me a few more minutes," his sister said, "and I'll have dinner ready for you. Sarah, a little help, please?"

"You don't have to feed me."

"I insist."

"Well, let me help you guys," he said. He came over, smiling, and helped prepare the rest of the meal, to Meghan's evident relief. She had never been the most brilliant chef in the family, so it was particularly touching when she tried to make a meal for company.

The meal was quite tasty: a baked ham with brown sugar glaze, served with scalloped potatoes, green beans, and perfect golden dinner rolls. Meghan had stepped up her game this time. She turned on some soft Christmas music to accompany their meal, then took her seat across from him.

"Sarah says you were quite a demon out there on the ice," Meghan said. "You really helped her get her confidence back."

"Ah, it was nothing—it was all her," Ben said. He shook an admonishing forkful of ham at his niece. "Don't try to rehabilitate my reputation, Sarah, it's a lost cause. You were the one who helped me stay upright when I stumbled and almost fell!"

The teenager grinned. "I know you only stumbled because you saw that lady."

Oh, no, what did I open myself up to? He glanced over in dread at his sister's face. She arched her eyebrows. "What lady, dear brother? Spill it."

There was no getting out of it now. "Just an old friend from school days. Allison O'Brien. She was out skating with a couple of her friends, and we chatted for a minute... she's arranged a meeting for Grandpa Skip tomorrow morning with a potential buyer for the bookstore, from New York." Ah, the perfect, rapid transition. "But I met the guy today, and he wants to change a lot about the place. I don't know that Grandpa Skip should sell to this stranger... what do you think?"

Meghan tilted her head. "He needs the money, right? Can't hack it anymore and he wants to retire. Why should it matter who he sells it to, as long as he gets a fair price for it?"

"So you wouldn't be upset if The Old Bookshop became... like, an ultra-hip social networking cafe or something?"

His sister laughed. "What does a 'social networking cafe' even mean? No, I mean... any port in a storm. Holloway Green could probably do with a business or two to bring it into the 2010s... or heck, the 1990s. Right now the town is living squarely in the past, and suffering for it. Bookstores are probably the past, not the future."

Ben shook his head. "You never were much of a reader, huh, Meghan."

She shrugged. "Why read when you can walk, ride, swim, fish, enjoy all of this natural beauty? I mean, I'll listen to an audiobook once in a while on my headphones, but... I don't know, who's even got time to read anymore?"

He put down his fork. "Come on! I refuse to believe that people aren't reading books anymore. And The Old Bookshop is an iconic part of Holloway Green."

"Maybe you should try running it, then, and see how it goes."

"That's what I'm thinking," Ben said quietly. He returned to eating his meal.

Meghan's mouth dropped open. "*You*? Running a bookstore? What if you decided to go off on Habitat missions again and left Grandpa Skip in the lurch?"

"I wouldn't do that," he said, wounded. "I'm here to stay. And I could do the job well, I *know* I could. I've already learned a lot over the past couple of years about the business and the book industry."

She touched his wrist briefly. "Sorry, didn't mean to insult you. I'm sure you'd be an excellent bookstore manager, Ben, if that's what you want to do. But is it? I've never heard you mention the possibility before, or anything like it."

"Maybe I... needed the right inspiration," he said. Unbidden, Allison's face came into his mind.

He must have blushed. Or maybe Sarah was just using her teenage superpowers of detection. But the girl said, "Ooh, I think it was that lady who got him thinking about it. I saw them talking—they seemed awfully friendly with each other. I saw sparks flying."

"No, come on," Ben said. "Allison has a boyfriend back in the city."

"Mom, there were sparks. I *saw* them."

He played his ace. Desperate times and all. "Say, Sarah, maybe you should tell your mom instead about the boy you met up with at the ice rink. The one with the purple scarf. Isn't that why you wanted to get rid of me after a few turns around the rink?"

Now Sarah was the one to blush.

Meghan sat up straighter. "*What* boy? Sarah?"

The conversation had been successfully diverted. Ben breathed a sigh of relief and just enjoyed his food for a few minutes, listening to mother and daughter banter back and forth. The two had grown even closer to each other in the years since Meghan's husband had died, forming almost a sisterly relationship. But on the subject of teen romance, Meghan still held some fairly rigid ideas.

"You're thirteen," she was saying. "Too young to hang out with boys unsupervised."

"Mom, there were people all around us, and Uncle Ben was right nearby…"

He stepped back in to rescue his niece. "They were just chatting for a minute, Meghan. It was completely innocent."

But, of course, Sarah didn't exactly look grateful for his efforts; he had been the one to bring up the mysterious boy in the first place. For the rest of the meal, she made a point of avoiding talking to him. *Ah, I'll have to pay for that later. Maybe in driving duty to the movies.*

After dinner, they tucked into a variety of delectable Christmas cookies complete with gooey frosting. Then, as Ben was getting ready to leave, Meghan sent her daughter into the other room to clean up some things, and took him aside on the little front porch.

"Sarah's no dummy," she said. "If she saw sparks between you and this woman… I believe her."

"It's nothing," he said, though he knew he was reddening again.

"If Allison really does have a boyfriend back in the city, just be careful," Meghan said. "I don't want to see you get your heart broken."

He put on a stoic look. "Me? I'm the toughest guy you know. I don't even have a heart."

She folded her arms and leaned against the doorway. "Yeah. Sure. I know you, Ben. You're one of the most senti-mental people in the world, deep down. That's the same reason you're even thinking about taking on The Old Bookshop yourself. It'd be just like you to reconnect with someone you went to high school with a million years ago and rekindle an old flame."

"No, no, there was none of that," he protested. "I never had feelings for her. If anything, she was into *me*."

Meghan's eyebrows raised still farther. "Allison used to have a thing for you?"

He clapped a hand over his mouth. His eyes widened. It had just come out without thinking, but... it was a reasonable assumption to make, wasn't it? Back in high school, Allison had always dashed away from him after saying like three words.

It changes nothing. Even if she had a crush on me back then, that was a long time ago—and she's attached now.

He huffed out an indignant breath, which immediately turned to frost. "No. I don't know. Who knows. It doesn't matter, does it? That was so long ago, it might as well be the age of the dinosaurs."

"That checks out," she said, quirking a grin at him.

"Come on now. You're the older sibling. Any jokes about the Cretaceous Era are just going to land back on you double." He was just teasing her; honestly, she looked younger than he did. She'd have suitors lined up to the town square if she ever decided to dip her toe back in the dating pool.

Meghan rolled her eyes. "All right, you'd better get back to your hovel before the snow gets any thicker," she said. "Thanks again for spending dinner with me and the kid."

He bowed. "Thank you for a top-notch meal. That's the best ham I've had all year."

"Drive safe!" she called after him as he approached his truck.

The snow *had* increased in thickness and regularity since he drove over here, but Ben took it slow on the way back and arrived home without any issues. Four-wheel drive definitely helped. *Wonder if Allison's got snow tires,* he wondered to himself as he trudged through the gathering snow on the sidewalk to his apartment, and then reminded himself, for the hundredth time, to get a grip already.

CHAPTER 7

*A*llison stormed into the living room and pointed a finger at Sam, who was sitting in an overstuffed armchair reading and relaxing after another long shift at Jackpine. "You," she said. "I can't believe you asked me to do that."

"So you talked to Evie?" Sam inquired sweetly, glancing up from the pages of his thick book.

"Oh yeah. And I think I've screwed up our friendship. I should never have agreed to try to sell her on your 'buddy' Ben." She sniffed at the air. "Is that popcorn?"

"Just made a big batch. It's over on the table. Want some?"

Her resolve wavered. "Well… yes. But I'm still mad at you. This changes nothing!"

She marched over to the table and found an enormous bowl of popcorn, made from kernels on the stovetop rather than a microwave bag, and freshly buttered and salted. She scooped a bunch of popcorn up and stuffed it into her mouth, then sat on the couch across from Sam.

He put down his book and picked up a mug of hot chocolate. "So… why? Why would setting them up screw up your friendship?"

"Evie's not ready," she said. "For her, emotionally, I think her divorce still hurts like it happened yesterday. And then I seemed like a creep trying to push a guy on her."

Sam made a face at her. "A creep? Really? What did you do, try to make them kiss?"

"No, but I may as well have. When I was talking about Ben to her, I sounded weird and desperate. Evie left in a hurry soon after we picked out a tree; she seemed in a much different mood than at the beginning."

Christine entered the living room then. She had one of those ridiculously large candy canes that Dad had over-ordered for the Jackpine Mountain lodge; apparently Dad had been pushing them on everyone. "What? Who's desperate?"

"I looked the part, anyway," Allison complained. "Because Sam here got me to try setting up Ben Whitfield with Evie."

Her sister looked to Sam. "That's not a joke? The two of them would make a terrible match. Sure, they're both incredibly good-looking, and technically available, but their personalities don't mesh. Ben would drive her crazy with his macho tendencies. That's exactly what happened with Ryan."

"Oops," Sam said.

"Yeah, *oops*," Christine scolded him. "Ben should be with someone who could cheerfully put him in his place. Like…" She fell silent.

Allison's heart beat faster. *Who were you going to say?* She groaned. "Evie didn't appreciate my matchmaking efforts," she said. She left out the part where Evie had thought *Allison* had a thing for Ben, because that would only complicate matters right now.

"Don't worry about it," Sam tried to say.

But again, Christine overrode him. "And *you*, genius, not

only tried to make a bad match, but also corrupted the process of Allison and Evie becoming friends again. Of course Evie would be ticked off at Allison. Just like if she'd discovered the reason Allison agreed to help her pick out the Christmas tree was so Allison could pitch her on a set of steak knives. Nobody likes to be *sold* to, Sam. Do you understand?"

"I guess." He seemed nonchalant, though he probably didn't want to admit he'd been wrong.

But Allison had been wrong, too, to agree to the setup attempt. *Especially since you have feelings for Ben yourself,* a little mental voice pecked at her...

"No, I don't," she blurted aloud.

Christine said slowly, "You don't... understand, or...?"

Allison cleared her throat. She had to press those feelings down, if they did exist. There was no point. Her life was back in New York. Which reminded her: she was the kind of person who could be wantonly cheated on and then kicked to the curb. Hardly a catch. "I don't... nothing."

Then, to her own surprise as much as theirs, she burst into tears.

Christine softened and went to put her arm around Allison on the couch. "What's wrong, honey?"

I can't hold it in any longer. She looked from Christine to her brother's concerned face, then came out with it. "Peter was cheating on me," she said, knuckling at her cheeks, though her tears were quickly replaced by fresh ones. "For months. He just broke up with me a couple of weeks ago... and he wasn't even going to tell me about the other woman until I forced it out of him." Then she added, though it felt unnecessary, "Someone from work."

"Aw, man," Sam said. "I'm so sorry to hear that. Next time I visit you down there, I'm going to track down this punk and kick his butt."

The thought of Sam, of all people, attempting actual violence made Allison giggle against her will. "Please don't. Don't hurt him, Sam."

Christine squeezed Allison closer to her. "What a creep. What an absolute waste of space. I can't believe it. You deserve so much better than that, I *promise* you, Allie." Then her expression clouded. "Why didn't... why didn't you tell us when it happened? Why'd you say that Peter was just too busy to come up and meet us?"

She hung her head, feeling a wave of shame crash over her. "I... I guess I was too embarrassed. And I didn't want to get the holidays off to a sad start. You guys all looked so happy and cheerful and, and in the Christmas spirit. I didn't want to throw sour milk all over that."

Sam wrinkled his nose at her metaphor and put his fistful of popcorn down without eating it. But Christine looked confused. "You know you can talk to me," she said, "can talk to either of us about anything. Thinking you'd spoil the holiday season by being honest with us, that's... just silly."

"And a little hurtful," Sam added. "I mean—"

"Shut up, Sam," Christine ordered. "This is not about your tender feelings. Allie's been through the wringer, when it's supposed to be the season of good cheer."

Then Christine straightened, and Allison felt a pang of dread at what she would say next. She hurried to cut Christine off: "No," she said, "I haven't told Mom and Dad yet either. I don't want them to be disappointed." *Or to say something that'll cut me to the quick.*

"Why would they be disappointed?" Sam said, looking confused.

But a knowing look came over Christine's face. "It's Dad. Right? You're thinking about... what he said when my fiance broke up with me."

Allison felt like curling into a ball and opting out of the rest of this conversation. "Um… yeah. I remember it clearly."

"Me too," Christine said glumly. "But he did apologize for blaming me for the breakup. I don't think he'd make the same mistake again with you."

Allison wanted to agree with her sister. Or to say, *Hey, even if he does, it's no big deal.* But she knew herself better than to pretend Dad couldn't make her cry all over again. "Maybe he won't," she said. She paused. "I promise I'll tell them tonight."

MOM AND DAD prepared a succulent roast beef dinner for tonight, before the official decorating of the O'Brien Christmas tree, along with an experimental cocktail for the Jackpine restaurant that Mom was calling "Christmosas." The name was still under debate.

At around seven, a knock sounded on the door, and Sam jumped up to answer it. He came back into the living room with a young blonde woman in tow. "Hey Allie! I want you to meet Sabrina. Sabrina, this is Allison, a high-powered publishing professional from the *isle of Manhattan*."

The young woman looked confused, but she offered a hand and said, "Hi. Nice to meet you." She looked like she had graduated from college this year—or perhaps was still taking classes.

Sabrina's handshake was limp and moist. Allison resisted the urge to wipe her hand on her pants. "So, umm, how did you two meet?"

"It's *such* a funny story," the young woman trilled. "I accidentally hit Sam's back bumper with my car. Well, the bumper, and the fender. The fender fell off. Sam said we didn't need to let the insurance companies know or anything like that, which was great, because my car insurance was a little bit lapsed, hee hee…"

Oh no. Oh… no. Allison glanced at Sam, who seemed mortified.

"Darling," said Sam, "I thought we agreed not to tell it this way."

She slapped his shoulder lightly. "But you're *such* a gentleman, how could I not talk about how, you know, gentlemanly you were? You said we could pretend it never happened if I let you take me out for a coffee, and I said *Sure,* but I only drink cappuccino frappes from the Coffee Hero at the mall in Conway. And the rest is… you know…"

"History?" Allison tried to ease her way away from the happy couple, back toward the couch. Christine entered the room then, behind Sam and Sabrina, and rolled her eyes at Allison. Allison winced.

"That's right!"

"I hear you and Sam bonded over a mutual interest in ghosts," Allison said. "Christine told me. Right, Christine?"

Her sister reluctantly joined her on the couch. "Yes…"

"Oh! Yes! Over the cappuccino frappes, I was telling Sam all about my many encounters with lingering ghosts and other spirits," Sabrina enthused, "and then Sam mentioned that he used to be into paranormal stuff when he was a kid. And it turned out all he needed was just a little encouraging from the right person to get back into it. I mentioned that *Finding Faraway Ghosts* was my favorite reality show, and we watched some episodes together on our third date. Our first date was going to the movies."

"The Harry Hogan movie about the—" Sam tried to break in.

"Twenty angry ghosts," Sabrina interrupted. "It was perfect. And then afterward, we went back to the Coffee Hero. I know it's like, basic, blah, right, everyone goes to

Coffee Hero everywhere in the country, but totally, they do *such* a good job with their..." She hesitated, looking off into the distance.

"Cappuccino frappes?" Allison said. The phrase became more meaningless the more she said it, and she was hoping she wouldn't have to again.

But Sabrina shook her strawberry blonde locks. "No, silly, I was remembering all the other great drinks they have there. They do a good job with their macchiato lattes, and an okay job with their cappuccino frappes, but you have to get them there because it's the only place to get *real* ones."

"Real cappuccino frappes?" Christine said.

Allison shot her a look, but Christine gave her an evil smile, as if to say, *You brought me into this.*

They could have gone on for hours in circles, but Mom marched in and announced that dinner was ready and she'd like some help setting the table in the dining room. Allison literally jumped at the chance, vaulting off the couch and going into the kitchen to grab some silverware. She hesitated when setting Sabrina's place, momentarily unsure whether the girl was old enough to drink one of Mom's "Christmosas."

Over dinner, Christine gave Allison a knowing look across the table. She knew it was time to tell her parents about Peter. She didn't want to, especially not in front of a random person—why did this girl Sabrina have to be here, now?—but she'd made a promise to her siblings.

"Mom, Dad," she began, taking a deep breath, "I haven't been honest with you about something."

Both her parents set down their forks and looked at her attentively. Mom's expression was a bit distressed, while Dad's looked shaded by irritation. *Ah, won't this be a blast...*

"Peter and I broke up weeks ago," Allison said. "He dumped me, and then after I weaseled it out of him, admitted that he'd been cheating on me for months with someone from his work."

Mom shook her head. "Oh no, I'm so sorry."

"I'm sorry, too," Dad said. "Sorry that you didn't feel that you could tell us. Why did you lie, Allison?"

Lie. That was a harsh word. Not exactly sympathetic. But she probably deserved it. "I didn't want to ruin the holidays," she said, addressing her dinner plate. "Everyone seemed so happy."

"It's all right," Mom said, casting a quieting glance at Dad. "We understand."

"I'm… not sure I do," her father said, not taking the hint. He tapped a finger on the tabletop in seeming agitation. "Why would being honest with us have ruined the holidays, while lying to us was somehow the Christmas spirit?"

"Dad," Christine said.

He blew out an angry breath, making the candle flames flicker. "I'm very sorry you experienced that kind of treatment from that guy, Allison. You should never be treated that way. I… hoped that we could all be truthful with each other. But—you living so far away, maybe you feel like you don't know us as well anymore." He paused, then added, "I feel like I don't know you as well as I used to."

She mumbled, "I'm sorry."

"Don't listen to your father," Mom said sharply. "Of course we know you as much as we always have—you're our daughter. Distance will never change that, or time."

"'Don't listen' to me?" Dad fired at her. "Yes, by all means, don't listen, because I know nothing. I'm just a stupid old man—"

"Franklin—"

"Stop it, both of you," Sam said, raising his voice louder than Allison had heard in quite some time. Even his girlfriend flattened back in her chair at the sound of it. "Did you forget we have a guest? This is completely embarrassing."

Sabrina tittered nervously. "Oh, don't mind me. Pretend I'm not here." Her reticence lasted for all of five seconds, then she said, "When my last boyfriend dumped me, it was a very painful experience. I felt like I couldn't even tell anyone about it." As Allison began to nod in sympathy, grateful for the girl's attempt to commiserate, Sabrina went on, "Of course, I was the one who had cheated on him, so I guess it was my fault in the end... but still, I felt very bad."

Allison sighed. She no longer felt hungry; she pushed her plate of roast beef away. Sam groaned as he looked at his girlfriend and withdrew his arm from her shoulders.

Christine spoke up, affecting a bright and cheery tone, "So is everyone ready to decorate the tree when we're done eating? I figure we could save dessert for when the last ornament is on the tree... tradition, you know."

Nobody responded. Dad shoveled food into his mouth mechanically. Mom abruptly got up from the table. "I'd better bring the boxes down from the attic," she said, and she hurried away.

CHAPTER 8

*C*elia Drake had owned the Winter Rose bed and breakfast for several decades, and it showed, particularly in the breakfast parlor. The decor was strongly influenced by old lady aesthetics, from the lace tablecloths to the dusty, flowery wallpaper and the scent of rosewater that had settled over everything.

So a man with Valentino Boggs's intimidating size and girth looked incongruous squeezed into a chair at one of the tiny breakfast tables, sitting across from Grandpa Skip. Boggs, today wearing a black suit over his massive frame, looked as though he might bust his chair at any moment and send the splinters flying.

As Ben entered the room, his first instinct was to laugh, but he wisely stifled it and offered a greeting to both men: "Good morning! Hope you saved me a scone or two."

He pulled over a wicker chair to the table and sat down carefully in it; he too would have to make sure he didn't break anything in here, though Boggs was much more likely to play the proverbial bull in the china shop. Boggs and

Grandpa Skip were both staring at him, the latter plucking at his white beard as if lost in thought.

"What are you doing here?" the New Yorker asked bluntly.

"Grandpa thought it'd be a good idea if I were here to bounce ideas off," Ben said. "Isn't that right, Grandpa Skip?"

The old man frowned, then nodded. "Yes. Apologies for not mentioning that part, Mr. Boggs."

"Please, call me Valentino," the big man rumbled.

"Er… right. So, *Valentino* and I were just discussing a very generous offer he's prepared to make me for The Old Bookshop," Grandpa Skip said. "Why don't you take a look at the sample contract he's drawn up, Mr. Ben? The highlighted line might be of particular interest to you."

He passed over a stapled set of papers. Ben took them and scanned right to the line in yellow, indicating the price that Valentino Boggs was offering for the bookstore. And his eyes nearly popped out of his head.

"I… *what?*" he whispered.

"I took the liberty of strolling around your quaint little village yesterday after our rendez-*vous*," Boggs said, his gravelly voice taking special care to enunciate the last word the French way. "I am, in a word… enchanted. I see multiple opportunities for growth in Holloway Green that have been squandered, but that could be easily nurtured by the right person. With The Old Bookshop as my capstone property, I am prepared to make substantial investments in other businesses and properties around town to bring unprecedented growth to the entire community."

So, in English, you want to buy up the whole town. "Why?" Ben asked.

Boggs lifted a tiny teacup to his lips and drank before answering. "I have lived in New York for too long. It is a…

cutthroat world. A small place. No room for expansion, and too much competition. I believe the future lies in communities such as Holloway Green. Someday soon, most workers will be able to perform their duties away from a physical office— technology will free them to work from anywhere. They'll flock away from the noise and grime and inflated prices of the *metropoli* to places like Holloway Green, to breathe fresh air."

Grandpa Skip gave Ben a cool look over the glasses that had slipped down his nose. "What do you think about all that?"

"I think… you would be a rich man if you accepted this offer," Ben said slowly. "But I also think you could be dooming the town to becoming Valentino Boggsville."

Boggs pursed his lips. "That's a bit of an exaggeration, don't you think? The town retaining its original character is of importance to me."

"Some would say Holloway Green is dying on its own," Grandpa Skip said, his tone even and dispassionate, as if he were working out something aloud. "Under the mismanagement and neglect of the mayor and the town council, in a difficult economy, and so forth. I agree with Mr. Boggs that you're overstating the 'doom' the town would face if he made some investments. But even say it were a choice between becoming a ghost town and becoming Valentino Boggsville, which one is better in the end, Ben?"

"It doesn't have to be a choice between those two options," Ben protested. "If enough caring, motivated people put their energy into revitalizing the town, we could turn things around. Recessions aren't forever. Bad leadership doesn't have to be forever, either—like, we could vote those folks out!"

The big man studied a scone, turning it over in his hands. "This has become a philosophical debate. My offer is a concrete thing, but its time is limited. You must let me know your decision the day after Christmas, Mr. Whitfield, or the offer will be withdrawn."

He got up. The chair beneath him groaned with the shifting of his bulk, and Ben was sure that snapping would come next, but the furniture held together. Valentino Boggs brushed past them and into the parlor; a moment later, the sound of piano music drifted through the doorway.

"Come with me, Mr. Ben," Grandpa Skip said, and let him out.

Outside, in the cold, Grandpa Skip's neutral expression dropped, to be replaced by a challenging look. "You could have warned me you were coming to the meeting."

"You weren't even going to tell me about it," Ben said. "I had to hear about it from Allison."

His grandfather sighed, letting out a frosty breath. "I wanted the chance to think it over for myself. I know you've been interested in running the bookstore for a while now, but it's ultimately up to me... and this Boggs told me that you said you were a candidate for *buying* the shop!"

"I did," Ben said, his defenses rising. "I—didn't like the way he was talking about changing it. Didn't like his attitude. And just now he proved to me that my instincts were right. He—"

"Listen, son," Grandpa Skip interrupted. "You shouldn't assume you have a claim on the property. It's not a birthright. There's a *reason* that I've never entertained your talk of managing the bookstore, and it's not just because I don't want to see you tangled up in a risky enterprise that could bankrupt you."

Ben felt even colder now than when they'd first walked out of the Winter Rose. He rubbed his hands together, cursing his lack of gloves, which were in his other coat. "What? What's the reason?"

"I'm... not certain that you'll be staying long enough to

make The Old Bookshop a success," Grandpa Skip said. "What if you decide to leave Holloway Green again? Take off for years on another humanitarian mission?"

"I won't," Ben said. He couldn't help but feel hurt by his grandfather's lack of trust in him. "I'm not going anywhere, Grandpa. When Grandma was sick, I realized I needed to come home. To be here with you, and Meghan and Sarah."

"Is it guilt that makes you stay here, then?" Grandpa Skip said. "Or worry about my well-being? You can see I'm doing fine. Your sister's doing fine. What's to stop you from leaving again? You're still young, unattached. There's a whole world out there—surely your old hometown has gotten stale by now."

Ben's heart wrenched. "Grandpa, I'm really sorry for being gone for so long. For so many years. I couldn't deal with... well, I wasn't facing up to my issues. But I've grown, and I—I love being near you and my sister and niece, and I think it's really important, but it's not my *whole* reason for staying. Holloway Green is a *good* place. I feel like I belong here."

His grandfather gave him a long look. Finally, he put a hand on Ben's shoulder and squeezed gently.

"All right," Grandpa Skip said. "How about a trial run?"

"A what?"

"Open the bookstore back up. You have until Christmas. See if you can sell enough books each day to at least pay for that day's heat and electricity."

Ben couldn't believe what he was hearing. He watched, stunned, as his grandfather fished a little notebook and pencil out of his coat pocket and scribbled a few calculations, apparently from memory, then tore out the piece of paper and held it out to Ben. "That's the grand total you'll need to earn to prove you can make The Old Bookshop a success.

Then we'll... reconsider. Otherwise I'm taking Valentino Boggs's offer."

I can do that. "Thank you, Grandpa Skip," Ben said. "Thank you so much."

Then he let out a whoop that echoed over the frozen town green. "I'm going to get the store ready to open *today!*"

"Yes, you'd better get cracking," Grandpa Skip said. "Santa'll be here before you know it. I'll help you get started, but the rest is up to you."

"Great!" Ben said. "I'll meet you over there!" Then he hurried down the street, toward The Old Bookshop.

He fumbled his phone out of his pocket as he went. He had to share the news with someone—and there was one particular person who came to mind.

BEN WAS busy for a long time in The Old Bookshop, first having to clean up a lot of materials and dust from his repair and renovation work. It was only now, late in the afternoon, that he could turn to the tasks of rearranging the book stock and decorating with a holiday flourish. Grandpa Skip had stopped by a while ago, and then left, saying he needed to go work on his mysterious "project." Ben realized now he'd been too optimistic in thinking he could get the bookstore back open for business today. But tomorrow could definitely happen, if he kept working hard.

He brought the Christmas, Hanukkah, Kwanzaa, and other winter-holiday-related books to the forefront, then went through the stock and selected some titles that he thought might make for good gifts for family and friends. He set up a table with all of these books near the front of the store.

Then he set up a Bluetooth speaker he'd brought over

from his apartment and set it to play holiday tunes. The sound didn't reach as far as he'd like, with the maze of bookcases muffling the noise, but anyone at least near the front counter could hear it.

"O Christmas Tree" came on and he started singing along as he brought out a big box of holiday decorations that he'd found in the back of the store.

"You can carry a tune," someone said behind him.

He turned to see Allison O'Brien standing in the foyer of the bookstore. How had she not triggered the bell above the door? Then he looked up and saw he'd disconnected the bell when he was hammering some loose nails back into place.

"In a bucket, maybe," he answered her.

Allison looked stunning, lovely in a fur-trimmed winter coat. He had to force himself to look away. She went over to the front counter and set down her purse. "So I was thinking about your efforts to spruce up this place for the holidays... well, it looks like you're doing a great job here so far, but I wanted to know if you could use some help."

"Oh. Well—yeah, sure. If you really want to. But aren't you on vacation?"

"Why does everyone keep asking me that?" Allison said, smiling. "Can't a girl hang some holly and tinsel on her vacation?"

He smiled back. "She sure can."

Then a new voice spoke up: "Hello?"

The Old Bookshop seemed to be a popular destination tonight. He and Allison turned to see a woman entering the bookstore. She was in her middle years, short—perhaps even under five feet—and stoutly built. She had greying red hair and a spray of fading freckles on her cheeks, and she looked friendly, albeit a little scatter-brained. She was carrying a thick book under her arm that she hadn't picked up from the shop's shelves.

"Hi," she said. "I'm Walters."

"Walter?" Then he realized she meant her last name. "Oh. Walters. What can I…"

"Hey there, Ben," she said, seeming to ignore Allison. "It's Ben, right? Skip's grandson?"

"That's right," he said. "We're not quite open yet, but—"

Walters let out a loud cough, as if clearing the way for her own speech. She said, "I have a question for you. Do you carry and sell books by local authors?"

Ben nodded. "Yes, Grandpa Skip has been keeping a little shelf over there with a LOCAL label on it. I'm not sure how long some of those books have been there, though. There was a coat of dust that I had to—"

"Great, great," Walters interrupted, and coughed again. The sound seemed to be automatic. She thrust the book that she was carrying at Ben. "This is the first volume in my fantasy series, *Dread Lords of the Dragon Deep.* I'd like to have copies of the book sold here. I'll tell people to come to The Old Bookshop to find my books."

Ben looked down at the heavy tome in his hands doubtfully. The cover looked like it was put together by someone with only a dim understanding of Photoshop, and the title appeared in Payprus font. He could barely read the author name (Layla Scott Walters), its color so poorly contrasted with the background. Ben opened the book and saw that the text was super tiny, crowded into the middle of the pages by ridiculously large margins.

"Well, I don't know," he said. "This…"

And then to his surprise, Allison nimbly plucked the book out of his hands and said to Walters, "Thank you very much! Ben and Grandpa Skip will have to take a look through this and get back to you."

"That won't be necessary," Ben said. The book looked like the work of a complete amateur. Carrying it would be a poor reflection on the bookstore itself, not to mention possibly opening the door to other weirdo authors.

"What he means to say," Allison broke in, "is that it won't be necessary for you to worry about following up, Ms. Walters. Ben will make sure that he and Grandpa Skip get back in touch with you promptly. Do you have a business card with your contact info that you could leave with us?"

Layla Scott Walters smiled. "Oh, certainly." She took something out of her shirt pocket and gave it to Ben. It was just her contact information written in pen on an index card. *This is really not helping her case.* Ben shot a look over at Allison, but she avoided his gaze.

"Thank you very much," Walters said, "most sincerely. I've been having some trouble getting into the regional market, so this would really be a great boon. I know my local fans would appreciate it. Season's greetings to you both." And she walked out.

"Oh, I'm sure she has legions of fans," Ben said, smirking.

"Ben." Allison clutched the book to her chest, like she was afraid he would pitch it into the trash. "You don't want to outright say no to folks like that. They're a part of the community—they deserve your consideration. And you never know, this could be a hidden gem. You know the old saying about judging a book…"

"Yeah, yeah," Ben said. "But the inside is just as bad as the cover. What kind of consideration am I supposed to be giving that? I don't want to use up shelf space with books that will never sell… you see how these local books have apparently been here for years? They've turned yellow!"

"Maybe they need to be given a more advantageous placement in the shop." Allison shrugged. "Why don't you let me take a little read through—um—*Dread Lords of the Dragon Deep*? I'll let you know if it's any good. If your instincts do turn out to be correct, then we'll have to politely decline.

Emphasis on *politely*. You want this to be a place that welcomes everyone, and at least show that you looked at the book."

If she was willing to start reading the darn thing, better her than him. "That's a good point," he said.

"Of course it is," she said, grinning. "I know what I'm talking about. Now, let's see what you've got in this monster box here."

She set Walters' book down next to her purse and knelt down to rummage in the box of decorations, pulling out long evergreen garlands and fistfuls of tinsel. "Wow. How old is this stuff?"

"Vintage, some of it," Ben said.

Then Allison's expression changed. Her mouth opened. She leaned further into the box and took out a smaller box, then carefully extracted a ceramic tree. It was studded with little Christmas lights that would be illuminated from within the tree if you unscrewed the base and put a bulb inside.

"Oh my gosh," she said. "My grandparents used to have one of these." She turned the tree around, holding it gingerly. "It… can take you off guard, you know? How the sight of some silly little thing can bring back a flood of memories all at once."

He knew exactly what she was talking about. He couldn't help but smile at the childlike joy suffusing Allison's face, making her look even more radiant than usual.

"For me, it's Grandpa Skip's model trains," Ben said. "He's the one who put all the time into crafting them and painting them, but they always make me think of my grandma. Grandpa Skip treated his trains as, like, museum objects, but Grandma insisted that I be allowed to touch them and play with them as long as I was careful. Whenever I'd come over to their house, she'd play with the trains with me. He called her 'the Conductor.'"

She gazed at him, her lips softly curving. "That's a wonderful memory, Ben."

He rubbed the back of his neck, suddenly feeling embarrassed. "Anyway... where do you think we should put the ceramic tree?"

"Oh, you have to put it on the sales counter and plug it in. Light it up every time you make a sale!"

"Good idea." He cleared some space on the counter, and Allison made a little ceremony of setting the tree up.

For the next couple of hours, the two of them worked together to decorate the bookshop. Ben was gratified to see Allison continue to loosen up as they strung evergreen garland around the railings and hung strings of lights from the tops of the bookcases. She seemed to be getting more comfortable around him, and was having as much fun as he was.

At one point she wound garland around her neck and shoulders, as if it were a stole, and lightly whacked him with the end of it. "*Dah*-ling," she said, "do you carry any titles on tax evasion for the extravagantly wealthy?"

"Personal finance shelf, nonfiction, loft level," Ben said without missing a beat. Then he asked with a smirk, "Are you doing an impression of a Holloway?"

"Oh, that's not nice," Allison said. "You're talking about our town's First Family. That's like insulting royalty."

"The sooner we get them off the town council, the better," he said.

She raised an eyebrow. "You ever consider running for a council seat?"

"No way. I've got my hands full here."

"Just saying. You've got the looks for a politician. Definitely enough intelligence. Practice some stump speeches, and you could be well on your way."

Ben took one of the garland she was wearing and gently unwound it from her. "The looks, huh?"

Now her cheeks colored. "Um." She scrabbled in the bottom of the decoration box and came up with some squat, rather hideous figurines with pointed hats. "So, these gnomes with the pinecone bodies. Where did you want these?"

He showed her mercy and chose to focus on gnome placement. She lightened up again, to his relief. As they continued to work, Allison ventured a few suggestions for Christmas-specific marketing, and he made some further adjustments accordingly to the placement of the book stock.

Finally, he took a drink of water and wiped some perspiration off his forehead. He'd never thought he could actually get hot in this drafty barn of a bookstore, but it had been a long day.

"What would you say to maybe taking a little stroll around town?" Allison suggested. "Getting some food? I don't have a curfew to get back to my parents' house... not until at least eight o'clock, anyway."

"What a wild life you lead," he teased her. Then he tensed, remembering Meghan's warnings not to let himself get hurt. *What about her boyfriend? Would he approve of us going out on a... date?* "Just a short walk. And food because our bodies require it."

She nodded, tapping her nose and looking at him curiously. "Yeah. Two friends nourishing themselves."

"Let me just finish up this one task," he said, stalling. He went back to his reshelving, his back turned to her, and debated whether he really should go out for even a little while with Allison O'Brien. He certainly wanted to—more than he'd even realized he would—but what about the faceless stranger back in the big city?

What are you worried about? Let the other guy be the jealous one this time.

He finished the reshelving—effectively moving the books back to the same position they'd been in—and then turned to Allison with a smile.

"All right, let's go," he said.

He closed up the bookstore behind them, and then the two of them began to stroll through the picturesque, snow-laden lanes and byways of downtown Holloway Green. The town had not changed much over the decades—or centuries, even. The streets were walkable simply because the development of the town predated cars.

Ben could almost close his eyes and imagine the previous generations of Holloway Green residents walking these same avenues, on a winter evening much like this one. His grandfather often mentioned that the town had started as an artists' colony, bankrolled by wealthy patrons further south who wanted to adorn their homes and offices with oil paintings of the White Mountains. Had the artists been preoccupied with capturing the mountains the whole time, or did they ever stop to portray the human-scale beauty of their own community on a night like tonight?

"Feels good to be out in the fresh air," Allison said, breathing in deeply, her brilliant blue eyes sparkling.

"Yeah, that bookstore could definitely use an airing out."

"That's not what I meant," she said, flashing a grin at him. "No, I could never get tired of the musty smell of books."

"Oh, it's *musty* now?" he ribbed her. "Suppose I ought to get rid of some of the moldering old titles, then. Though Grandpa Skip says some of the books in the 'special collection' section are quite valuable, if you can find the right buyer."

"The 'right buyer' being anyone with sufficient money to blow on old books?"

He nodded. "Sure, though I'd hate to sell them to someone who's just going to lock them in a vault, using them as an investment."

"I agree," said Allison, sounding a little surprised. "Books need to be read and loved, not just… kept on the shelf. Especially not if the shelf is behind a titanium steel door."

A lazy drift of snow swirled over them, just enough to be atmospheric without being annoying. Ben gazed up happily at the dark sky—it seemed vast and impenetrable, an impossible source for the tiny little specks of whiteness.

"The air always did feel different here," he said. "Fresher. I've lived in places all over the country, and none of them ever had the same feel to the air that the White Mountains did. Or Holloway Green in particular, I should say."

"Public works pumps out the really good air during the holidays to make people shop more, I hear," she said with a wink.

"Where do they get it?"

She pretended to consider the question. "Bottles. They bottle it on the crispest, clearest days during the rest of the year."

Ben enjoyed this silly flight of speculation. He could picture the preposterous little bottles of air—in his mind they looked like plastic bottled water, but they *floated.* "Guess that department really earns its keep every year."

He thought he detected more than a trace of nostalgia as Allison looked around. Tiny snowflakes kept melting on her eyelashes.

"Do you ever get sick of the big city?" he ventured. "Miss small-town life?"

She stopped walking, seeming to genuinely consider the question. "I mean… yeah. Sometimes it can feel lonelier in the city than it does in a little place like this. You don't really *know* the people around you, though there are millions of them. It's like being a bear in a stream teeming with fish—you swipe out your paw, and maybe you can catch a few as they're swimming by you. But most keep coursing on by."

"Maybe swiping with your claws just isn't the best way to make friends," he said, sincerely amused by her choice of metaphor.

She laughed. "*Everything* moves so fast in New York—you have to be aggressive to grab what you want. But… sometimes it feels like everything's moving fast enough to leave you behind."

He sensed a vein worth mining. He rubbed his gloves together and said, "Do you feel like you're getting left behind down there?"

Allison hesitated, then let her shoulders fall. "Okay, yeah. I think I told you I'm basically a go-fer as an assistant editor, with only occasional opportunities to do the work I'm really drawn to. I'm supposed to be more advanced by now—some of my peers have taken leaps ahead of me. But they've had to put in a ton of extra unpaid hours, suck up to people like Jerry, make personal sacrifices to get ahead. It just seems… a little empty."

"Jerry?"

"My soulless goblin of a boss."

"Ah," he said. "Jerry is a good name for a goblin. But… I thought you loved working in the book publishing industry."

They wove a path through the light layer of snow on the sidewalk. "I love working with authors," she said. "Helping to shape books to match their creators' vision, and to reach a wide audience who will fall in love with their words. But I just don't get to do *enough* of that; too much time is taken up by other stuff, some of it petty, some of it driven by real business concerns. It all doesn't add up to the same thing as loving books… you know?"

He nodded. "I think I understand." On the tip of his

tongue was the wild suggestion *Quit your job and move back here,* but he bit it back.

He abhorred the thought of Allison being in the big city feeling alone and feeling empty at her job. Whoever her boyfriend was, he was clearly falling down on the job of helping Allison find a more enriched life.

"Maybe you should," he started to say, letting his guard down, and then clamped down on the words.

She raised her eyebrows at him. "Sorry, what were you saying? Maybe I should what?"

"Oh, no. I successfully stopped myself from giving unqualified advice. I'm just here to listen, Allison."

She worked an apparent kink out of her shoulders. Her scarf rose with the motion, exposing a pale sliver of the smooth skin of her neck. He stifled an irresponsible impulse to kiss her there. "No, go ahead," Allison said. "At this point in my life, I don't even know what 'qualified' means anymore… I'm open to ideas from all quarters."

Nervously, he tugged at the sleeve of his winter coat. "Oh. I don't know. Just wondering if there's some alternate route in your field you could take toward working directly with authors more. And cutting out some of the other aspects of the business that you're not in love with."

Allison nodded at him, breaking into a gentle smile. "That sounds like a perfectly qualified suggestion to me, Ben. I appreciate it, I do." She tilted her head. "Some folks might make that kind of job description happen by becoming agents. But I know I'm not pushy and nervy enough to be an agent."

"I bet you could be pushy if you gave it a shot," Ben said.

"Thanks…?"

He'd been steering them toward Desjardins' Diner, his stomach rumbling at the thought of a big plate of poutine.

Now they came around the corner and the diner came into view. He pointed at it. "Hey, do you want to…?"

A strange look came over Allison's face then. "Oh—no. I —I'm not quite hungry yet. Why don't we…"

She glanced around them, though Ben wasn't sure what she was looking for. Then she said, a little loudly, "Hey, look at that! The holiday horse-drawn carriage is there. I've kind of always wanted to do that ride, but was too embarrassed to be seen doing it. Like, people would think I'm a tourist or something."

This was an abrupt change of course. He looked over at the carriage. "Uh, yeah. The horses are from my sister's farm. I could probably tell you their names if I got a little closer."

"Then let's get closer," Allison said brightly, and she took his arm and tugged him toward the carriage. He went along , enjoying the feel of her arm linked with his. Though he was still suspicious without knowing why.

"So… introduce me," she said when they came up to the carriage. The driver, wearing a top hat and old-time garb, peered down at them curiously as Allison ignored him and went right to the horses.

Ben inspected the horses, two beautiful chestnuts. The one on the left he recognized due to the distinctive star pattern on its muzzle, but the other one was slipping his mind. "This is Silver, and this is… Stinky. Guys, this is Allison O'Brien. They're both delighted to meet you, I'm sure."

"Stinky? Really?" Allison said.

"That's Beatrice," said the driver, with a reproachful look at Ben. "Are… you folks interested in taking a ride?"

"Yes. It's on me," Allison paid him and climbed up on the seat, then offered her hand down to Ben. "You're coming, right?"

He laughed. "Uh. Yeah. I don't need a hand up, though. He

clambered up the side of the carriage and sat down next to Allison. Their thighs were close enough to touch. He sighed, taking pleasure in her nearness, the warmth of her.

Be careful, his sister's voice admonished him in his head. *And leave my horses out of it.*

CHAPTER 9

They took a slow, scenic ride through the downtown area, Allison snugging up against Ben. He didn't pull away. She was so thankful that he'd gone along with the carriage ride, weird and sudden though the idea had seemed, and they'd avoided the chance of running into Evie at Desjardins' Diner. What would Evie have said if she saw the two of them come in together? Would she have thought that Allison brought Ben in to continue to push him on her?

Disaster averted. She let herself relax.

"Ah, I love all the lamps lit up, with their wreaths," she sighed. "And the candles in shop windows and in people's houses... it's like the look that New York goes for during Christmas, but it's *real.* Authentic."

"You *are* a tourist," he teased her.

"Am not."

"Just listening to how you're talking about Holloway Green and its realness, a cozy little town during the holidays, like you didn't grow up here. Like you're an anthropologist. And soon enough you'll be back to the big city and forget about all of us all over again...."

She looked at him seriously. "I won't. I… never have. Holloway Green is always in the corner of my mind, no matter what I'm doing in the City."

"As an idealized piece of nostalgia?"

"Maybe sometimes," she admitted. "But—mostly I miss my parents and my brother and sister. As I get older, being closer to them seems more and more important to me."

"Older, huh," he said. "You must be the ripe old age of thirty-two right now, if you were two years behind me in school…"

She cocked her head, surprised. "So you remember what class I was in, huh? I must not have been *completely* invisible to you."

"No," Ben said. "Not invisible at all. I wished back then that you would talk to me more. You just seemed so… interesting."

"Always what a girl wants to hear," she said dryly.

"I mean it, though. So smart, probably full of fascinating insights from all those books you read—but you'd barely give me the time of day. Always running away from the beginning of every conversation."

"I was… intimidated," she said. No way would she tell him that she'd had a crush on him back then. "You were, like, one of the kings of high school. You always seemed like you had it together."

Ben gave her a smile tinged with sadness. "Might have looked that way on the outside. But inside, I was pretty messed up. My mom had died from cancer a few years before that. And then… my dad left us. Left Meghan and me. Meghan was several years older than me, so maybe he thought that she could take care of me from then on."

She stared at him, genuinely shocked. She couldn't believe that she hadn't known that, the way gossip traveled in a small town like Holloway Green. His grandparents must have gone to great lengths to protect the children from the often vicious consequences of the rumor mill. "That's horrible."

"Yeah. I don't know where he went—I don't know where he is now, either, or if he's even still alive. But his parents, my grandparents, stepped up in a big way. They took care of my sister and me. I think that Grandpa Skip and Grandma felt responsible for their son's awful choices. To this day, I don't know if my father has ever gotten in touch with Grandpa Skip... I never wanted to ask. Still don't."

She felt a terrible guilt come over her, for how she'd yelled at Ben for interfering with Valentino Boggs's visit. He'd been trying to protect the grandfather he loved. His desire to carry on Grandpa Skip's legacy and run the bookstore had even more poignancy to her now.

She took his gloved hand in hers, and looked deep into his rich brown eyes. "Ben, I'm sorry. No wonder you're so close with Grandpa Skip. I had no idea about any of that."

"Well, it's ancient history now," he said. "It doesn't matter anymore. I still have family members who love me, and that's what's important."

She asked, hesitantly, "Was that the reason that you were away from Holloway Green for so long?"

"Yeah. As soon as I was done with school, I couldn't wait to put this place behind me for a long, long time. Everywhere I went in Holloway Green, all I could see was the ghost of my mother. And the memory of a man who gave up the title of 'father' and made his kids into orphans."

Allison leaned into him. "But you came back..."

"I did," Ben said. "When I found out my grandma was sick... was dying. I had this terrible feeling in the pit of my stomach—I realized that I had been just like my father. Repeating his same exact mistake. I ran away when I couldn't deal with my feelings. So I knew I had to get back to be with Grandma during her final days.

"And then I wanted to stay."

Allison gave him a soft smile. "It's not such a bad place to be. A lot to offer, if you know the right people."

He stiffened and drew away from her. He pressed himself against the interior of the carriage door. "Anyway. That's enough wallowing around in the past."

Allison looked away, a little hurt. But she thought she understood. It was raw territory to revisit, and… *I let myself cozy up to him too much. It made him uncomfortable.*

"Let's catch up to the present," Ben said, with a false-sounding cheeriness. "I'm sure you're full of fascinating insights from all those books you read, and I can't wait to hear them."

"Yes, that's me," Allison said.

But a silence fell that neither of them could quite break for the rest of the carriage ride.

As they walked away from the carriage, Ben said, "I just realized how late it is. I've got to get some sleep and then get up early to make sure I'll be ready for the store reopening. Grandpa Skip is going to meet me there… early. So I've got to go."

I thought you were hungry. She certainly was, after all the work they'd put in at the shop. But she wasn't going to push it.

"Don't worry about it," she said. "Friend. I—thanks for hanging out tonight, and good luck with the grand holiday reopening tomorrow. I'll try to swing by."

I'M SUCH AN IDIOT.

Allison kept having that thought as she returned home,

the refrain drowning out greetings from her family members as she walked through the door. Mom offered her a glass of egg nog, but Allison shook her head and locked herself in the first-floor bathroom, attempting to collect her thoughts.

What madness had possessed her to ask Ben out on a little "night on the town"? He had seemed so... well, handsome, especially when wielding tools, and she had been feeling lonely. She'd thought it would do no harm to hang out for a little while.

And then... their conversation while walking around had drawn them closer together. A lot closer. And she'd felt the tingling throughout her body that she had felt whenever she ran into Ben Whitfield in the high school halls, all those years ago. She'd let her old crush on him resurface just when he was sharing personal, painful information about his family, and he must have sensed it.

Did I seem like I was throwing myself at him? He'd said he wanted to be friends back in high school too; he'd never hinted at a reciprocal romantic interest. So of course he wouldn't be feeling anything of the sort *now*.

"Good lord, get it together," she said aloud, slumping against the door.

"Hey, are you all right in there?" Christine said, sounding close to the other side of the door. "Allie? Allison?"

She sat up, scrambled away from the door, and faced the bathroom mirror. She looked on the verge of tears. "I—I'm fine," she called back. "Just... ate something that didn't agree with me."

"Well... if you need me, let me know." Her sister's doubtful voice faded.

Allison wrung her hands together. Perspective. She was still too raw after getting dumped by Peter. Even flirting with a guy was a bad idea right now. Especially when she'd just be heading back to the City in the new year.

She blew out a noisy breath, staring at herself in the mirror and willing herself to get under control. She ought to be focusing on spending quality time with her family; it was Christmas, and she only had a limited number of these days.

Allison exited the bathroom and went to the fridge, where she discovered the slice of bûche de noël that Sam had taken home from the diner. He'd apparently forgotten about it. *Mine now. He owes me anyway.*

She put the cake on a plate and then joined the other O'Briens in the family room. Most of them were either half-asleep or napping, but Dad wasn't; he gave her a half-questioning glance as she sat down. But he said nothing.

She and Dad had been on cordial terms since last night's tumultuous dinner, but hadn't spoken about much of anything at all. Allison would have to make an effort to patch things up later; tonight she just felt tired. She picked up the mug of egg nog that Mom had left for her; it made a fine complement to the Yule log cake.

THE FOLLOWING MORNING, Allison was up and in the kitchen early. Mom was getting a big supply of Christmas cookies ready and welcomed Allison's help; Dad was working at Jackpine Mountain for the day. Both Christine and Sam were off on their own errands, probably some late Christmas shopping.

Allison worked the dough on a fresh batch, glancing over at her mother as Mom got some soft piano music going and then turned on the oven. The sun streamed brilliantly into the kitchen, made stronger by the reflection of the snow layer outside that refused to depart.

"You and I haven't gotten much chance to talk alone until

now," Allison said. "I'm glad for it... I wanted to ask you something."

"Sure, honey," Mom said faintly. She greased a pan with butter.

"I know you were defending me against Dad the other night, and I appreciate it," Allison went on, "but I'd like to hear your honest thoughts. Are *you* disappointed in me for not being honest right away about Peter?"

Mom shrugged. She didn't meet Allison's eyes. "It's fine. It doesn't really matter. I just want you to be happy, Allison. Your own relationship business isn't really our concern, unless there's ever anything that you want to, or need to, talk about with us."

Allison shaped the dough into little balls on her pan. "I mean," she said, "I know you were probably hoping I'd be settled down by now with somebody. Working on some grandkids. I'm the oldest, and—"

"Stop that," Mom said sharply, looking around at her.

She was startled. "Stop what? What am I doing wrong?"

"Putting words in my mouth," Mom said. Now she did look annoyed, but not for the reason Allison had expected. "You're my daughter, not a grandchild factory. Have I ever made you think otherwise?"

"No," Allison admitted. "But—"

"That sounds like your own insecurity talking," Mom said.

Allison jerked back as if she'd been slapped.

Noticing her expression, Mom's face softened, and she was quick to add: "These are all ultimately your own choices, and I support you either way. I wish I could have comforted you the minute that awful man broke up with you and said those hurtful things. But you're an adult. You..." She paused. "You probably didn't *need* me. And I understand that."

Allison put down the dough she was working on and

rushed over to her mother, putting greasy hands on her shoulders and squeezing her in a hug. "Oh, Mom," she said. "I'll *always* need you. I'm sorry to make you think otherwise."

Her mother gripped her back, hard. "Ah, don't pay attention to me," Mom murmured. "I'm just getting sentimental in my old age!"

Finding herself laughing, Allison drew back and patted her mother's shoulder. "Never stop being sentimental. I don't plan to."

"Well, then... there's still an opportunity for you to cry on my shoulder over Peter, if you'd like."

She smiled. "No, it's all right. I'm over it."

"Are you sure?" Mom said. "You may still need closure. My recommended solution is to call him on the phone and use the most awful epithets you can think of."

"I'll... keep that in mind. But I don't think I need that kind of closure."

"Everyone needs closure," her mother said. "But let me ask you something, dear. As long as your father isn't around to steer the conversation. Are you truly happy in New York? I mean, the breakup with Peter aside—just your life there. Your career. Is all going like you hoped it would?"

Allison paused, intending to answer her mother honestly. She thought back to the conversation with Ben last night, when she'd confessed to feeling stuck in her job. Ben had suggested she try to think of alternative paths that could get her closer to what she really wanted, but... that was easy for him to say. She could admit, though, that her life in the big city, in the publishing world, hadn't exactly turned out the way she had envisioned it.

"Honestly... no," she said. "I don't want to sound like I'm complaining about my job, but..." She spilled the contents of her heart to her mother, much as she had with Ben, though with a more hopeful note this time; even as she was talking, she realized that she *could* make changes if she had to. Her life was hers to control.

"I think you're courageous for jumping into that field," Mom said when Allison had finished unloading. "It sounds fairly stressful and cutthroat. But your father and I will always respect and support you, no matter what you choose to do. You don't *have* to keep struggling to be the next... the next..." She paused, looking puzzled. "Can you name a famous book editor for me? Right now I'm drawing a blank, I'm sorry."

"The next Max Perkins?" Allison offered. "Worked with Hemingway, Fitzgerald, a bunch of other legendary authors. He's from a long time ago..." *That should tell you something.* "I guess most book editors these days don't get to be so high profile."

Mom nodded. "Well, you don't have to be the next him or anyone else. I want you to follow your heart, dear, but don't give up your soul along the way."

It was sage enough advice. "Thanks, Mom. I appreciate you saying that." *What is my heart even trying to lead me toward these days?*

CHAPTER 10

*I*t was early when Ben arrived at The Old Bookshop on the day of the reopening—though not as early as he'd insinuated to Allison. Grandpa Skip was there already, casting a critical eye at the rearrangements and the decorations.

"You put your heart into this," he observed, adjusting his glasses.

"I did," Ben said. "But I had help."

He went to the front counter, feeling fresh excitement at the challenge ahead of him. Grandpa Skip had, reluctantly, gotten a tablet-based card swiping system set up not too long ago. Ben reactivated it, made sure there was some change in the till for cash customers, and went around and turned on all the festive lights, throughout the store and in the front windows. He felt energized and excited, ready for anything.

Grandpa Skip took a seat in one of the comfortable old armchairs, then gestured at the front door. "You might also want to flip the sign from 'CLOSED' to 'OPEN.' Just a thought, Mr. Ben."

Ben chuckled and went to the door. Talk about the more-than-symbolic gesture that would make this official. He turned the cardboard sign around to the other side—then opened the door and stepped out onto the sidewalk.

"The Old Bookshop is open for the holidays!" he shouted.

A few passersby looked at him as if he were crazy, then continued walking. Cars didn't stop; no one stopped. A teenage boy on the other side of the street shouted back, "End capitalism now!"

Ben stood, blinking, in the winter sunlight, then went back inside. *What, did you expect everyone to suddenly come running toward the store?* He had a good laugh at himself, then sat on the stool behind the front counter. Grandpa Skip exchanged a look with him.

Minutes stretched by. Then an hour. Ben realized he had practically fallen into the screen of his own smartphone, so intently had he been looking at it. Grandpa Skip was leafing through a medieval history book and sipping on a tea; he looked up and said, "Did you fall asleep?"

"Might as well have," Ben admitted. He put the phone into a drawer and closed the drawer. Looking at the news and social media certainly hadn't helped to calm his nerves about the grand opening.

"Did you send out an e-mail to the customer list?" Grandpa Skip inquired.

"Oh, uh..." Ben reddened. "I forgot."

"You just thought once you turned the sign around, there'd be a stampede to the front door!" Grandpa Skip scoffed, then indicated the front counter. "The information for logging in is on a piece of paper taped to the bottom drawer. Why don't you let folks know. It's not a big list, but..."

Ben nodded. "Yeah, of course." He got out the bookstore computer and consulted the login information, then went into Grandpa Skip's newsletter service. Grandpa Skip hadn't been kidding—there were under a hundred people on the e-mail list. *This is barely going to make a difference.* But he drafted a quick, enthusiastic e-mail and then hit send.

Ten bounce-backs immediately landed in his inbox. Of course Grandpa Skip hadn't sent out an e-mail in a while, and some people had switched addresses; the list was going to be even smaller than Ben had thought. *Fingers crossed it brings in* somebody, *or I'm gonna look pretty foolish to Grandpa Skip...*

He waited another fifteen minutes. He realized he'd just been assuming that people would kind of show up because A) it was the holidays and people needed to shop, and B) locals had been badly missing The Old Bookshop. Condition A still held, but what if Condition B had been him fooling himself? *Believe in the bookstore.*

Grabbing a feather duster, Ben went around and wiped off minute specks that had gathered on shelves here and there, up on the balcony level. Then, he heard the bell over the door tinkle. He dropped the duster and sprinted down the stairs to see an elderly woman standing just inside the door of the store.

"Do you sell vacuum cleaners?" the elderly woman said, addressing her question to Grandpa Skip rather than Ben, though his grandfather clearly had his nose buried in the book about the Middle Ages.

"No," Grandpa Skip said shortly, not bothering to look up.

Ben stepped forward, putting on a broad smile. *"But,"* he said smoothly, "we do sell books about housecleaning. And I think we even have a biography of that guy who designed a super-efficient vacuum. Not to mention a philosophical nonfiction book about what it means to be 'home.' Would you be interested in any of those?"

The elderly woman shook her head. "Don't have time to

read. I have to watch my stories on the TV. Are you *sure* you don't carry vacuum cleaners?"

"We don't," Grandpa Skip said, waving his hand while still not looking up. "You want the Vacuum Village three doors down, Frida. It looks nothing like this store, you can't miss it."

Frida, the elderly woman, said, "Thank you, Grandpa Skip," and left the store, the bell announcing her exit.

"You see, she even knows my name and still can't remember that this is a bookstore," Grandpa Skip said cheerfully. "Batty old dame."

Ben couldn't help but laugh, though he was still disappointed that *that* had been their first "customer." "You shouldn't talk, Grandpa Skip."

"Get ready for a dozen more Fridas," Grandpa Skip said, putting his book down. "People who come in and say that they can't remember the author or title of the book they're looking for, but they remember the cover is *blue.* Or they want the perfect gift book for someone who hates to read. Or… they come in, sit down with a book, read it for an hour, then put it back on the shelf and go buy it from the Internets instead."

Ben didn't want to encourage his grandfather, so he just said, "Hmm."

"Do you sell board games here?" the old man went on. "Do you sell olives? I want the movie version of this book. Is there a kids' version of *Twelve Years a Slave*? Of *The Flowers of Evil*? Can I get this in a comic book version instead?" He snorted.

"All right, I get it," Ben said, annoyed. "Some silly people will come in. That doesn't negate everyone else who does love to read."

Grandpa Skip grunted. He sat back in his chair, patted at

the unruly white tufts of his hair, and resumed reading and drinking his tea.

And then the bell tinkled again, and a trim blonde woman walked in, looking around. Evie Desjardins, who worked at the diner. He recalled going to school with her, though she would have been in Allison's grade or maybe a year older.

"Hi," she said, smiling at Ben. "Are you guys open? For real?"

"For the holidays, at least," Ben said. "Thank you for coming in, Evie! How can I help you?"

She tucked her hair behind her ear and looked away from him shyly, heading instead for the nearest bookshelf. "I've been slacking on Christmas gifts for my kids," she said. "One is five, and the other's eight—I'd like to get them some books. Do you have anything appropriate for their age?"

"Yes!" Ben said, feeling a surge of relief that she had not yet mentioned vacuums, or olives for that matter. "Follow me to the kids' section. We've got a nice breakdown of books by age range, though if your oldest is an advanced reader, you might want to consider bumping up a year or two..." He thought back to the research he'd done on kids' books, anticipating it to be a big part of the holiday market. "Or so I've heard, anyway."

She smiled at him and together they went over to the children's section of books, Ben forcing himself not to look over at Grandpa Skip to see his expression. He pointed out the different age ranges, and then was relieved to see that Evie went ahead and explored them herself; he didn't really have much more advice to give beyond that.

After a few moments, Evie had found three titles for each of her children. She tucked the stack of books under her arm and smiled at him. "These will be wonderful. Thank you."

Ben led the way back to the register. The tablet had fallen asleep, and he couldn't get it to wake up with the password

Grandpa Skip had given him. *Ugh, bad timing.* He tried the same password again... this time it worked. He'd just had fumble fingers. Apparently he was more nervous than he'd thought.

He totaled up the book costs. "We can take credit or cash, Evie, whatever works for you."

She paid for the books. As he was slipping them into one of the paper bags he'd found under the front counter, Evie said, "I'm so glad this place is open again. Holloway Green has really been diminished by not having a bookstore to visit."

"Well, it's just a trial run for the holidays," Ben said. "But yeah, tell your friends to do all their shopping here." He grinned at her and turned on the lights on the little ceramic Christmas tree that Allison had placed there. *Sales!*

"Don't lay it on too thick," said Grandpa Skip from his cozy armchair.

Evie laughed softly and waved at him. "Grandpa Skip, now that you've passed the torch, you can't boss him around too much."

Grandpa Skip gave her a thin smile but didn't bother to correct her.

"What was your inspiration to open the shop back up?" Evie asked Ben.

He tried to banish Allison's face from appearing in his mind, yet it did anyway. The lit-up ceramic tree on the counter didn't help. He shrugged. "Had help from an old friend. Turns out, being pushed to sell this bookstore made me want to encourage Grandpa Skip to hang on to it." He lowered his voice and added, "Now I just have to prove it's worth keeping in the family."

Evie nodded sagely. "And was this old friend Allison O'Brien?"

He froze at the mention of her name, then tried to warm

himself up again. It was a small town; everyone talked to everyone. It didn't mean anything that Evie knew that he and Allison had been working together on the fate of the bookstore. "Yeah… as it happens."

"She thinks very highly of you," Evie said.

As a friend. So long as the guy back in New York was in the picture, nothing else would ever happen. That realization had come back to Ben with a crashing force last night, in the carriage with Allison. He couldn't let himself get drawn into a false hope, so he'd withdrawn from her and fled after the carriage ride, stuffing his face back in his apartment.

"Thanks, that's… nice to hear." Then he paused, looked at her curiously. "She was talking about me? To you?"

"Oh, she… just during the course of conversation," Evie said, turning awkward. She'd been on the verge of saying more, but now she clammed up. "Anyway, thanks so much for your help with the book selections, Ben."

He nodded. "Next time you two are talking about me, I'll know it, because my ears will be burning!"

His stupid joke fell flat. Evie's expression was blank. "Yeah… sure thing. Well, good luck with the holiday sales!" She marched out of the bookstore with her bag of books for her kids.

Grandpa Skip gently laid down his thick medieval history book and peered at Ben through his thick glasses. "Mr. Ben. Son. What was that all about?"

Ben wrung his hands together, now thoroughly mortified. "Nothing. I—I thought at first that Evie and Allison talking about me could be a good thing. Then… it occurred to me, maybe not so much." *Well, at least I made some sales.*

The bell over the door startled him. Someone else was coming in: Mrs. Yates, from the toy shop. "Hello, you two," she said warmly. "I heard the bookstore was back open!"

Mrs. Yates ended up buying two books, and to Ben's

surprise, a steady stream of new customers soon followed her. Some of them had gotten the e-mail he'd sent out to the list, but others had actually noticed the lights in the windows and the sign being switched to OPEN. Ben was kept busy looking up books in the catalogue and running around from shelf to shelf, and eventually Grandpa Skip was drafted back into service when multiple customers needed help at the same time.

As the end of the business day neared, Ben was tired but gratified to see just how many books they'd sold. They were on fire already!

A final pair of customers nosed their way through the door before closing time: two O'Briens, as it turned out, Allison's brother and sister. Ben considered Sam a friend, but the guy barely acknowledged Ben, offering just a quick wave and seeming distracted. As Sam ducked his way toward the nonfiction bookshelf devoted to legends of ghosts, goblins, and so forth, Christine O'Brien clapped her hands at the sight of all the Christmas decorations and the special displays.

"Wow! You've done such a great job getting this place in shape for the holidays!" she said.

"Thank you," Ben said, smiling. "I did have a fair bit of help from your sister yesterday—I have to say Allison really made a difference."

"I bet she did," Christine said. "Thanks for keeping her busy... honestly, I'm sure she got as much out of it as you did. She's been having a hard time settling down and relaxing on her holiday break—needs an outlet for all her energy."

"She *does* have a lot of great energy," Ben said. *Careful.* "Anyway, what are you looking for?"

"It has to do with Allie, actually," Christine said. "I'd like to get her a book. Do you have anything that would... um... convince her to move back here?"

Ben gave her a suspicious look. "Books on mind control, is that what you're looking for? Or perhaps the fine art of persuasion?"

She shrugged. "Ah, I don't know. I want Allie to get all misty-eyed over small-town life and decide that she belongs back here after all. Is that so much to ask? Maybe there's a novel or something that would get her in that kind of mood."

"Wouldn't hurt to try, I suppose," Ben said. "C'mon, I'll show you where the cozy small-town mysteries are, maybe something like that. Maybe we can even find a cozy series set in New England… do you happen to be familiar with any of these authors?"

He went with her to the cozy mystery section and they browsed through the books for a few minutes. As he read the backs of some of the brightly colored novels, he couldn't help but open his fat mouth again: "Do you think she would *want* to move back here? Like, not just because a book got her all, um, misty-eyed?"

Christine sighed. "I mean, I'm being selfish, but it doesn't seem like she's all that happy back in New York."

"Yeah, I got that sense as well," Ben said.

Christine raised an eyebrow. "Have you guys talked about her life in New York?"

He sensed he was entering dangerous territory. "A little bit. I mean, here and there."

Allison's sister nodded and then picked up a novel, seemingly at random. "I think this one will do."

"You sure?"

She nodded and took it to the register. He followed a moment later, and found that Sam O'Brien had been waiting for the two of them there, with a stack of books about purportedly real-life hauntings. Ben's eye wandered over the titles: *Ghosts Caught on Film* by Melvyn Willin, *Passing Strange* by Joe Citro, *New Hampshire Book of the Dead* by Roxie

Zwicker, *Ocean-Born Mary: The Truth Behind a New Hampshire Legend*, by Jeremy D'Entremont...

Christine rolled her eyes. "Surprise, surprise. One-track mind."

"I hadn't realized Grandpa Skip had such a great selection of books about ghosts," Sam said. "Unless you ordered those for the store, Ben?"

"Nope, not me."

As Ben rang up the total, Christine went on: "Sam, you've gotta broaden your horizons."

"That's no fun," her brother said with a wry smile. "What else could there really be to life besides supernatural phenomena and ski slopes?"

"I'm serious," Christine said. "Like, I know you work hard at Jackpine, and Mom and Dad are grateful to have you on staff. But you're obsessed with ghosts, you're still living at home, and you're dating college students... don't you feel like your development is a bit, um, arrested?"

"Come on," Sam protested, "Sabrina already graduated college." Then he added, reluctantly, "Earlier this year."

"Ah, give the guy a break, Christine," Ben put in. "I'm sure he's saving a lot on rent."

"Exactly," Sam said.

Christine sighed dramatically. But she winked at Ben to show she was giving her brother a hard time.

Then he shook his head, as if clearing a fog, though he still seemed hesitant to look Ben in the eye. "Hey, man, I just want to say... nice work getting this place up and running again."

"Tell you all about it over an adult beverage," Ben said. He considered Sam O'Brien a friend, if not one of his closest. "What are you up to tonight?"

"Oh... family stuff. Holiday stuff. Family holiday stuff." Sam straightened, cast a nervous-seeming glance at his sister.

"But some other time. Soon. Well, we better get going, Christine."

"Thanks for your help, Ben," Christine sang out as she flounced away. "Good luck with the Christmas sales!"

Ben noted the time—past closing. He went and turned the sign around on the front door, then began to tidy up around the bookstore before counting up the day's sales. Grandpa Skip joined him in the effort.

"Starting tomorrow, you're on your own," Grandpa Skip said, clapping him on the shoulder.

CHAPTER 11

The day of the big Holloway Green holiday parade had arrived.

Allison wished she felt more excited about it—it was usually a highlight of her visit home for Christmas. But she'd still turned out with her family to offer their hand to any last-minute tasks that still needed to be done, then watch the parade on Main Street.

She'd seen that The Old Bookshop was indeed open today; Christine and Sam reported that it had been open yesterday, as well. She knew she should stop in and buy something, but hadn't yet found the courage. She kept thinking of Ben opening up to her, and then thoroughly shutting down.

Practically the whole town had turned out to celebrate, and many of the big, garish floats celebrated the cherished institutions of the town, including local businesses. She'd helped her parents drag the Ski Lodge Float out of the shed for its annual mounting on Dad's pickup truck. Now Dad was behind the wheel, his truck in the lineup of floats waiting for the signal to proceed.

Sabrina, Sam's girlfriend, had turned out for the event as well. She was currently on Sam's arm chatting a storm into Allison's ear about some multi-level marketing scheme. Allison would have preferred to talk about Sabrina's belief in ghosts, or really anything else.

"And you wouldn't believe some of these leggings, Allison. I saw a pair the other day that would look just darling on you. What are your feelings on animal prints?"

Allison gritted her teeth. "I… con. Definitely con when it comes to animal prints. Sorry."

Christine whipped her head around, nearly spilling her cup of hot chocolate. "Did someone say animal prints?"

Sabrina's eyes gleamed with avarice. "Would you excuse me a minute, Allison? Christine, hon, let's talk…"

Allison let out a deep breath and let herself relax, scanning the crowd for familiar faces. Across the street, she spotted Evie and her two kids, and the sight made her think, *I still need to apologize to her. That's something else I've been putting off.*

Evie caught her eye. She gave Allison an awkward smile and looked away.

Another missed opportunity, but Allison wasn't ready to give up. She belatedly raised her hand in a wave, trying to get Evie's attention. Then, too late, she saw that Ben and his grandfather were standing almost directly behind Evie, just outside the door of The Old Bookshop. Ben was looking at her. He clearly thought, as she met his gaze, that the wave was meant for him, because he raised his hand to her in return, wearing a puzzled smile.

Just stop it, she scolded herself. Allison turned her attention to her mother, standing nearby. "So, Mom…" she said, grasping for a suitable topic, "who do you think they're going to crown Miss Christmas?"

Mom smiled and said, "I think Katie Townsend is a shoe-in. I just hope she's ready to change into her gown…"

Then the trumpeting blew, signaling for the parade to begin, and everyone cheered. Mayor Beaulieu stood up at the podium and said, "Ladies and gentlemen, welcome to Holloway Green's annual celebration of the winter holidays! I hope everyone's brought their holiday spirit, because we all have a lot of cheering to do! Let's wish a Merry Christmas, Happy Hanukkah, and most Blessed Kwanzaa to everyone who put in hard work to make this parade happen!"

They cheered and clapped for the parade workers. Then the mayor said, "Let the parade begin!"

And the high school marching band started up, and the floats moved down the street to much joy and cheering, as well as phones poking up above the heads to take pictures. Tony's husband Jorge, waving and honking, drove a police cruiser to represent the town force. Allison watched floats go by representing the general store, the outdoor gear shop, Desjardins' Diner, Yates' Toys, and Lawson's Tree Farm, and then cheered especially loudly for the Jackpine Mountain float being piloted by her father. "Yeah, Dad!"

Her father grinned at her, throwing her a salute as he went by. Allison put a marshmallow tree in her mouth and washed it down with hot chocolate. Ah, this was the life.

It occurred to Allison that Ben should have tried to get a last-minute float for the bookstore, and an announcement from the mayor that they were temporarily open for the holiday. She was sure that Mayor Beaulieu would have been open to the idea. *Oh well, at least they can take advantage of the foot traffic and welcome people in…*

She felt a sudden tremor in her arms and legs and fought to get it under control. She managed to do so by the time the last of the floats had gone by. The crowd filtered into the street, which had turned into a temporary pedestrian zone to encourage everyone to congregate, shop and, well, be merry.

"Mind if I split off for a bit?" she asked Mom.

"Go ahead, dear. We'll just be down at the food truck in front of the general store. Your father is going to meet us there after he parks the truck." Mom bobbed her head at Allison and then moved away with the rest of the family.

Allison went over to The Old Bookshop; the old man had gone inside, but Ben remained at his station just outside the door, on the sidewalk.

"Hi," Allison said.

"Hi," he said back. He looked especially handsome today, with his cinnamon-colored coat complementing his eyes, but his expression was guarded. "Have you been... enjoying the parade?"

"I have," she said, tucking her hair behind her ear. "I was thinking just now—you guys should have gotten a float in the parade."

"I asked Grandpa Skip," Ben said. "We do already have one from previous years in storage. But he refused... said he wanted to see how sales go *without* any big advertisement in front of the whole town. Said it'd be cheating."

She giggled. "So, then, how are sales going without the 'cheat' of a parade float?"

"Pretty well! Started slow and then we had a big rush of people. Not many folks in this morning, but I think everyone was just getting ready for the parade start—I expect some people to start coming in now."

As if on cue, a young couple brushed past him and through the doorway of the bookstore. Ben gave them a considered second or two of polite distance, then whispered to Allison, "Excuse me, I've gotta make this sale happen!"

"Always be closing, isn't that what they say?" Allison

replied. But Ben was already dashing off, doing his best to pretend to just casually be near the couple as they browsed the selection at the front, in case they had any questions.

She went inside too. She wanted to buy something as at least a small gesture of support. *I do have a number of folks on my gift list I need to take care of.* Allison strolled along the shelves, aware that Grandpa Skip was watching her like a hawk from the balcony, a book forgotten in his lap.

As she looked through the displays of glossy books by the narrow stairs, each promising its own unforgettable adventure, her phone rang. Distracted by the titles in front of her, she absently put the phone to her ear, expecting one of her family members chiming in with updated plans.

"Allison?"

The confident male voice was unmistakable. It was Peter.

So dumb of me. If I'd only looked at the number calling... She pursed her lips and said in a harsh tone, "What do you want?"

"Baby, please just give me a minute to talk. I know I don't deserve it, but—"

"One minute. I'm setting my watch now." She wasn't, of course, but it felt good to say.

"All right." Peter's words spilled out in a rush. "Listen, I made a huge mistake. I should never have gotten with Kim in the first place. Not when my heart belonged to you. And then I treated you so badly, and I've been kicking myself ever since—"

"Kick harder," she advised him.

"—and I want to make things right, if I can," he bulled on, oblivious to interruption. "I can't believe I screwed up everything we had together, threw away all of the time we spent... that was some of the most meaningful time in my life, babe. I just—umm, I want you back. I'll do anything to get you back. Can I come and see you?"

"No," she said immediately.

"I'm gonna be in Brooklyn tonight anyway, and I thought I—"

"I'm not even *in* Brooklyn right now," she said. Then realized her mistake.

"What? Oh. Ohhh. That's right. You said you were going up to your folks' place for the holidays. Ah, how could I have forgotten that? I think it's because I'm just distraught about us no longer being together. Listen, I have an idea—"

"No," she said sharply. Loudly. "I'm not interested in your ideas." *Stop it, quiet down!* She lowered her voice, embarrassed to think that anyone could have heard her yelling. "Or you, anymore. You might *think* you feel bad, but... even if you do, I feel worse. You broke my heart. Even if you..." Then she stopped. "Wait, you told me you were cheating on me with *Julie* from work. Who's *Kim?*"

"Oh, uh..." Peter faltered. "It doesn't matter, baby. All I want is you now."

"Don't call me again," Allison seethed, and she hung up the phone.

She looked around. Yep, everyone in The Old Bookshop was definitely looking at her right now. Including Ben Whitfield, whose mouth had dropped open.

"I'm... I'm so sorry," Allison blurted to the room at large, and then ran for the exit. She managed to smack herself in the face with the door in her haste to exit, and staggered with her body halfway onto the sidewalk, her nose ringing in pain. She was about to bruise herself a whole lot more if she fell—

Then strong arms were holding her, helping her back up. She blinked away tears of pain and saw that Ben had caught her before she could tumble onto the ice.

"Are you okay?" he asked gently.

"Yeah," she breathed. "Thanks to you. Oh man, I'm a mess..." She turned her face away from him before she could burst into tears.

He made sure she was sturdily upright before releasing her, then continued to gaze at her with those beautiful, concerned eyes. "What... what happened on the phone call? Who was that?"

"Someone who should never have called," she said, giving her head a sharp shake. She covered her face in embarrassment briefly with a mitten, then said, "Ben, I didn't mean to cause you any trouble. I hope my outburst and, uh, antics didn't just cost you some sales."

"Are you kidding?" he said with a grin. "Look, nobody's left the store. If anything, they seem even more interested in buying a book. I should frame it as a free show with every purchase. Can you repeat your act at 1 and 3 pm?"

"That's not funny," she said, sniffling. "You shouldn't make jokes about a woman in distress."

Julie and *Kim*... She'd met Julie a time or two at Peter's after-work social events, but had no idea who this Kim was. She supposed she didn't want to know. It didn't matter.

But it still hurt.

She abruptly turned away and said to the wall, "Hey, I should get going. But... congratulations on all your success so far. With the bookstore. It's going great, and..."

Allison felt her voice breaking and was thus forced to flee, walking quickly and only just preserving her dignity by preventing herself from running. Besides the lack of running, it was a sharp, unwelcome reminder of her high school days. Nerdy Allison, buried in a book and unable to summon the courage to deal with life outside its pages.

Argh!

Ben was calling something after her, but she couldn't hear it, so wrapped up was she in the hot flames of her embarrassment. She only dared glance behind her when she'd gotten a block or so away; thankfully, he hadn't pursued her, though he was still watching her anxiously. She gave him an awkward wave and then turned her face forward again, with the vague notion of seeking out her family.

She remembered a moment later that Mom had told her exactly where to meet them, and so she went there in a hurry, wiping her face against tears that never actually came. She composed herself fairly well by the time she saw the group, with Dad approaching them from a different direction.

"Dad," she said, "you did a great job in the parade!"

"All I did was drive my truck," he said, shrugging, but he gave her a tentative smile. "Is everything okay, honey? Your gloves are on backwards."

She looked down. The thumbs were indeed facing in the wrong direction, outwards, as if she were a freak of nature recently escaped from a lab. She fixed them sheepishly. "Everything's fine, Dad."

But she caught a look pass between him and her mother. Before she could try to reassure him further, Christine and Sabrina went up to her, arm and arm, and said simultaneously, "*Leopard print!*" Then they both laughed.

Allison was baffled. "Is that some kind of code word, or…?" Then she remembered the fatuous discussion from earlier, when Sabrina had been trying to get both sisters to buy her commissioned goods. "Oh no."

"I just ordered some leopard print leggings," Christine said. "Wouldn't you know it, Sabrina has an ordering app right on her phone."

Allison detected a note of sarcasm that Sabrina completely missed as she flashed her smartphone at them, grinning.

Christine went on, "You should get a matching pair, Allie.

Then we can be twins on Christmas Day. Sabrina says that if we order now, they should arrive here by Christmas Eve day."

Has she lost her mind? Allison captured Christine's other arm and leaned in to hiss, sotto voce, "Why are you doing this? Why are you doing this to *me*?"

"The kid's nice enough once you get to know her," Christine murmured back. "Sort of. Just do her a favor, all right? It's Christmas."

And that was Christine to the core: kind to a fault, even if it meant buying ridiculous items of clothing from a friend that she would never actually wear. Except this time she had trapped Allison into her folly too. Allison looked over at Sam, who was watching the three of them with a fond gaze, as if it pleased him greatly that his sisters were getting along with his girlfriend. Allison sighed.

"All right, sign me up," she said to Sabrina. "I think I'd take the same size as Christine. And if they don't fit," she added, shooting a sharp look at her sister, "Christine could just keep them."

Sabrina squealed and jumped up and down. "Another happy customer! You got it. Oh, I only take SparkleCash, is that all right? You do have an account with them, right?"

"Sparkle what?"

"It's what the kids are using to pay each other these days," Christine put in helpfully.

Allison frowned. "But what about the other app? I already have three other payment apps on my phone..." So this was what it was like to advance in years.

They spent a little while longer that afternoon enjoying the holiday festival that followed the parade, with many delicious things to eat and drink, and Allison caught up with several old friends she hadn't seen in quite some time. She noticed, as she was looking around, that there were in fact *too many* familiar faces; with all the work that the townsfolk put into the parade and festival, they should have attracted more people from out of town, maybe even out of the region. *Holloway Green has a long way to go. I've got to take the mayor aside one of these days...*

As she had that thought, she realized with a surge of relief that she'd recaptured her present-day self, brimming with confidence and competence. Her insecure bookish high school self had been banished once more to the back of her mind. *She can stay there for good, as far as I'm concerned.*

Finally, it was time to go back home and enjoy yet another tasty family dinner. They had an aunt and uncle who were coming over, and so Mom was in a bustle of activity; Allison was happy to lend her a hand and be of use.

She didn't think again about the call from Peter until later that evening, when she was cradling a steaming tea in the cozy little armchair in her bedroom. The nerve, the absolute presumptuousness. Yes, it was definitely a good time to take off from men altogether, and reevaluate things.

She looked out the frosted window at the plump, rising moon, then back down at the tea in her hands. It was an excellent evening to get some of her promised reading done. She reached for the fat fantasy novel by the woman who'd come into the bookstore the other night, Layla Scott Walters, and opened it.

Dread Lords of the Dragon Deep. A patently ridiculous title. And the text was so tiny that it gave Allison eye strain. She read:

Before he was a Lord, Leonhart of the Riven Hill had to content himself with being a Knight. Strife was the Rule in the Five Angels' Lands, rather than the Exception, in those days, and many were the occasions for Sir Leonhart to prove himself in battle in service to his King. But the surest trial of Leonhart's soul came not on the battlefield at all, but on a lonely, wind-battered mountaintop in mid-winter...

Before long, she was totally wrapped up in the story. By the time she looked up from the pages, it was the middle of the night, and her tea was ice cold.

CHAPTER 12

*B*en kept thinking back to the phone call. Permitting himself to *hope* there was a chance, like a foolish, lovestruck teenager.

He'd been working too many hours at the bookstore; that must be the real reason why his brain was so muddled right now. Not the unforgettable woman from his childhood who had seemed to be breaking up with her New York City boyfriend right there in his store, over the phone…

Oh, lord. Make it stop. But he'd heard enough of the conversation, her side of it at least, to draw reasonable conclusions, hadn't he? Allison had said she didn't want him, whoever it was on the line. She wanted to be left alone. And she'd been extremely upset afterward. If that hadn't been a breakup, what else could it have been?

He closed up the shop, put on his coat, and went outside. It was particularly cold this evening. He took a little walk through the path wending through the field that ran behind the general store. Civilization in Holloway Green dropped off fairly quickly, turning into the runup to the surrounding White Mountains and forests.

She's single now. You could make a move, if you feel the way about her that you think you do...

"Nah," he said aloud, releasing a plume of frozen breath. "I couldn't. I don't want to be *that guy*. She only just had her breakup, if that's what that even was, so..."

His phone buzzed and he looked down. It was a text from Sam, apologizing for being so spacey when he'd visited the bookstore the other day, and wanting to get together for a coffee when Ben was done with work.

Sam's timing seemed nothing short of opportune, now that Ben thought about it. Ben had been making so many assumptions about Allison's availability and relationships all along; he needed to get down to the truth of it. He could ask her brother.

I want to be with Allison.

The realization was strong and clear, like one of the December winds currently battering him. Maybe it had been from the moment that he saw her again after all those years, at the bookstore; maybe even a sliver of it had been born back in high school. But Allison O'Brien was foremost in his thoughts and wishes, and he felt like he'd just had the wind knocked out him.

Better hope for a Christmas miracle, he thought. *Even if she's interested in dating you, she's still heading back to the big city after the holidays. Where there are a million men far more accomplished than you are, Mr. Whitfield...*

Allison was still hurting from her breakup and he wanted to respect her feelings. He'd make plans to spend more time with her, but as a friend, at least for now. Then, if she was open to more, they could explore that. But what *would* be a good occasion for getting more time with Allison?

His sister's Christmas party, he realized. She'd invited a bunch of friends and colleagues, not just family members. It would be an ideal event to invite Allison to: meaningful but not too intimate, and offering them plenty of opportunity to talk.

He shot off a quick text to Allison asking if she were available tomorrow, trying not to put too much thought into the wording.

And then he whistled as he walked down to the Grounds for Celebration coffee shop with his hands in his pockets. Upon entering the warm, fragrant space of the shop, Ben looked around for Sam O'Brien, finally spotting him at a table in a quiet, dark corner of the place. Sam had a steaming cappuccino in front of him.

"Hey, Sam," Ben said in a jovial tone. "Can I get you anything to go with your cappuccino?"

Sam raised an eyebrow. "Maybe a… No, I'm good."

"You sure?"

"Okay, how about one of those buttercream cupcakes," he blurted. "Darn, I can't control myself. One with a chocolate reindeer on top, please."

Ben smiled. "No shame in that, and no problem. I'll be right back."

The barista, Izzy, greeted him with a shy hello as he ordered a black coffee and the frosted monstrosity that Sam had requested (surely Sam didn't intend to eat that whole thing by himself). Ben was distracted during his order; he kept glancing down to check his phone for a response from Allison. When he came back with the coffee and buttercream cupcake, Sam was hunched over the table, staring dully at the featureless surface.

"What's on your mind?" Ben asked. He sat down.

"First of all, cheers," his friend said, raising his cappuccino and clinking it against Ben's hot black coffee. "We've almost survived Christmas—just a little longer to go."

Ben quirked a grin and took a sip of his coffee. "What's there to survive? It's the most wonderful time of the year."

Sam shrugged. "For some. Me, I can't seem to get any peace—either I'm working crazy hours at Jackpine Mountain, or my girlfriend is dropping another not so subtle reminder about the items on her extended Christmas list."

"Extended?"

Sam gulped down some of his fancy drink. "Yep. Since she just graduated college this year, she's made an especially large amount of requests to Santa this year. Needs a few extra things to move out on her own and do her own thing. Are any of these things necessary, though?" He grimaced. "Not quite…"

Ben flashed a grin. Sam's new girl was a handful. Definitely too young for Sam, if only because he needed someone *more* mature than him to counterbalance his own immaturity. "Tell Sabrina hi for me next time you see her. And don't hold back on treating her right. If she's a recent graduate, she does deserve it, at least in this economy…"

In this economy, eh. He sounded like Grandpa Skip now.

"So, I wanted to come clean about something," Sam said, stumbling over his words. "I… a few days ago, I asked my sister—Allie—to set you and Evie Desjardins up."

Ben reared back. He hadn't been expecting *that.* "Huh? What? Me and Evie?"

What had Sam been thinking? He took a deep breath, trying not to get angry. In an even tone, he went on, "Sam… my dating life is my own business. We're buddies, but—why would you overstep like that?"

Sam tapped the side of his cappuccino cup. "I don't know what got into me. I guess I was just thinking that with the holidays upon us, you deserved to have some company. Hated to think of you being lonely, while I'm getting snug with Sabrina and everything. I know you're a teeny bit jealous of our relationship. You don't like to hang out with us."

"Jealous? Of *you*?" Ben sputtered. "You're delusional."

"That seems a little harsh," Sam said.

Ben fumbled for words. He was having trouble grasping them. He couldn't ask Sam about his sister's availability *now*. "I don't recall ever asking you to set me up with somebody."

"I *know*, I'm really sorry. I shouldn't have done it. Allie got pretty mad at me after I made her talk you up to Evie when they were hanging out. She—"

"*What?*" Now he was even more dumbfounded.

"Like, to see if Evie might be interested in you," Sam replied reluctantly.

"Oh, lord, are we back in middle school?" His face flamed with embarrassment. Now Evie coming into the bookstore had quite a different flavor to it, in retrospect. What if Evie Desjardins thought he'd *asked* to be set up with her? This was excruciating.

"I mean, she said no. Evie did."

"That makes me feel *so* much better." Ben cradled his head in his hands. "Why did… why'd you do that to Allison, anyway? Put her in the middle like that?"

"I guess I thought she could be persuasive. She's so confident, that… well, anyway, I guess it kind of screwed up the friendship that she and Evie were rekindling with each other. They used to be really good friends back in the day, you know."

Ben understood quickly. "But now Evie thinks Allison was buddying up to her in order to butter her up for *me*. Eesh. Sam, I'm trying to prove to my grandfather that I can run a business downtown. I can't get a reputation like the town weirdo. Evie *came into my store!* And I had no idea all this was going on."

He thought back to their conversation, trying to sift through it for any newfound significance. Evie had asked him what he thought of Allison. Maybe she was trying to get an idea of why Ben would supposedly go to Allison as a romantic go-between. Oh, this was so not ideal.

Sam threw up his palms, looking more annoyed than contrite now. "Hey, man. I'm sorry, but… I was just trying to help. You've been lone-wolfing it for so long that I thought—"

"You thought I should 'dive back into the dating pool,' with a little help from an old buddy?" Ben asked acidly. "I don't—I don't just go on dates with random people all the time like you do. I actually put thought into it. I've been biding my time for the right person."

"Random, huh?" Sam's expression clouded. "Weren't you just telling me to be good to Sabrina? You think *she's* random?"

Ben let a scoff slip. "I mean… come on, dude. Why do you think I don't want to hang out with you and Sabrina? She's torture to talk to. I don't have a clue what you see in her."

Now Sam got up from the table, scowling at him. "I don't have to sit here and take you insulting me *and* my girlfriend. I brought you here to apologize to you about the setup thing. Mission accomplished, so… I'm outta here."

"Hey, c'mon, Sam," Ben said. "I didn't mean it, I was just ticked off at what you…"

It was no use; Sam had already stormed out of the coffee shop, leaving his half-drunk cappuccino on the table. Ben shook his head, feeling bad about how the conversation had ended, but still having trouble getting over Sam's ill-conceived idea of the setup. Now his confidence in Allison having interest in him *personally*, rather than as the object of a pairing with someone else, disintegrated. Sure, they had a great conversation while decorating the bookstore, and later in the carriage, but…

"Hey, Ben," the dark-haired barista called out to him from

the counter, then came over and placed a hand on his shoulder.

"It's okay, Izzy," Ben said, shrugging, "everything's fine. I know I look a little down, but I…"

"You haven't paid yet for your coffee or the cupcake," Izzy said, a little awkwardly. "I didn't want to insist, when you were up at the counter, but just… you know, before you leave. I'd get in trouble with my boss otherwise…"

Ben sighed. Yep, his head definitely wasn't on straight right now. "Sorry, Izzy." He surrendered his credit card, then felt a buzzing in his pocket.

It was Allison, texting that she was indeed available tomorrow. *Sounds great, friend!* she'd added.

He sagged. If she were so willing to set Ben up with someone else, there was no way that she could have any interest in him herself. Sam O'Brien had destroyed his hopes. But Ben had to follow up now with the invite to the party anyway; anything else would be sour grapes.

THE O'BRIEN RESIDENCE was a nice house, almost an "estate," far more well appointed than anything Ben's family had ever been able to afford. Jackpine Mountain had brought in some lucrative dollars for the O'Briens over the years, even if it was past its prime now. Ben looked down at his semi-decent dress shirt, suddenly feeling inadequate.

His insecurity only increased when Allison O'Brien stepped out her front door, giving him a glimpse of an exquisite red dress just before she closed her thick winter coat around it. She looked like she was ready to attend an exclusive Manhattan book release party, or something. However, he noted with appreciation that she was sensible enough to wear sturdy boots with the dress—heels would have sent her tumbling on the ice. Perhaps skidding right into Meghan's barn. The thought made him smirk.

"What's that look for?" Allison said as she got into the car. "No secret jokes… you have to tell me."

Well, she asked for it. "I was just picturing you sliding on the ice into my sister's horse barn."

"Did you promise her I'd provide entertainment for the party?" she replied archly. "That was irresponsible of you. I don't perform the ice-capades for free. Although, *you* do, from what I remember of your skills over at the ice rink…"

"That was an isolated incident," he said with mock indignation.

"Anyway…" Allison said, her tone becoming more reserved. "How are things over at the bookstore?"

"Great. Sales are still pretty good, though they've been dropping off in the last couple of days." He drove on through the night, noticing a few flurries that hadn't been in the forecast. Hopefully the weather wouldn't turn too treacherous. With New England weather, you just never knew…

Allison peered at him carefully; he noticed. "Are you approaching the sales goal that Grandpa Skip challenged you with?"

He nodded, choosing his next words with caution. "I think so. It's going be tough, though, if the numbers dropoff continues."

Then he found himself annoyed again, thinking of Evie coming into the bookstore, the secret she'd had, the embarrassment that Sam had laid on him. Why hadn't Allison ever told Ben about trying to set up him and Evie? He decided to throw out a little line, to test her.

"How's your friend Evie doing?" he asked. "Do you think she's having a good holiday season?"

He sensed rather than saw Allison's guard go up, her demeanor stiffen. "I thought you talked to her more recently than I did," she said. "When she came into The Old Bookshop and bought some books."

She'd caught him there. "Ah, just wondering if you ladies had been hanging out again recently."

He'd overplayed his hand; Allison was now looking at him with more than a little suspicion.

"Hanging out *again*?" she said dryly. "Did I talk to you about hanging out with Evie the first time?"

"Um. You must have. When we were decorating the bookstore."

"I must have," she said. "Right."

Ben realized his mistake—Sam was Allison's *brother*, after all, and probably had told her about his confession to Ben about the setup. She had to know that he knew that she knew... ugh, this type of intrigue was not Ben's forte at all.

Allison said, after a carefully considered silence, "I'll be sure to tell Evie you say hi, the next time I see her."

Yep. Not off to a great start. The blowing curtains of snow parted soon after to reveal Meghan's property, with several cars already parked along the sides of the long driveway and both the house and barn adorned with cheerful, blazing Christmas light strings. Ben paused to wonder, briefly, what trials awaited him at this party before he hopped out to open the door for Allison.

But she'd already opened her own door and was standing out in the growing snow uncomfortably, shifting from foot to foot and casting him glances of frank distrust.

CHAPTER 13

*A*llison entered the party thrown by Meghan Whitfield a few steps behind Ben, who had charged ahead to enter his sister's house before her, forgetting to hold the storm door open for her and nearly letting it slam back in her face. *Nice going, Romeo,* she thought with a touch of annoyance—though she was already irritated enough.

Why had she agreed to attend this party with Ben? Suddenly the reasonable voice in her head who had urged her to accept Ben's invitation now seemed like a bad influence. Sure, Allison had figured she could use the opportunity of the party to connect with a few more folks from Holloway Green that she hadn't seen in a while, make up for the time she'd let slip away, as she had with Evie. And maybe encourage Ben to do a little subtle research into the book preferences of locals, because she wanted to see him succeed.

But... it seemed he'd had an ulterior motive in asking her to this party. Not romantic interest, as she'd initially suspected—and maybe even allowed herself to hope for, a little, though she knew she shouldn't be encouraging him in that direction—but taking her to task. Since she'd had the temerity to try to set Evie up with him. That seemed to be the subtext of their conversation on the ride over here.

I already apologized to Evie, she thought. *I shouldn't have to apologize to him too... he didn't even know I was doing it at the time. And this is all Sam's fault, not mine!*

She hovered in the entrance near the coat hooks, almost considering calling herself a rideshare to exit the party before even entering it. But... no, she wouldn't drag some poor driver out here in the middle of a gathering snowstorm.

Just deal with it. Make nice with everyone, and get Ben to take you home early. You can do that much, right?

She could. She was a fully functioning adult, after all, and she wouldn't let silly drama get in her way. She shrugged off her coat and hung it up with the others, then fairly charged into the farmhouse kitchen. There were a number of guests present there, chatting and enjoying hot beverages and snacks. Allison saw Ben talking quietly with a pretty, dark-haired woman in her thirties with a faint physical resemblance to him; that must be his sister, Meghan. She was supposed to be his older sister, but she looked younger than he was. Definitely a good-looking family.

Ben waved at her and said, "Hey, Allison! I want you to meet the hostess of this fine shindig."

"Oh, it's a shindig, now," Meghan said, rolling her eyes. "That's what I always aspired to." She offered her hand to Allison, who had reluctantly approached. "I'm Meghan Whitfield—I know we must have crossed paths before, Allison, I just don't remember when."

"It's a small town," Allison said, shrugging, and giving her a weak handshake. Meghan's strong, calloused hand gripped hers more firmly in response, and Allison winced. "I've been away for a while, though."

"Yes, Ben tells me you have a big-time publishing job in

New York," Meghan said, her eyes bright with interest. "That must be so exciting."

"It's… it definitely keeps me busy." She tried to remember the last time she'd been *excited* at her job, instead of just stressed out and feeling overworked. It had been a good while, it had.

"And do you have a big-time boyfriend down there too?"

Ben's eyes widened and he swatted his sister's shoulder. "Hey, wow. That's super rude, Meghan. Allison, I'm really sorry, I—"

"It's okay," Allison said. She unwillingly flashed back to the other day, when she'd been on the phone with Peter and embarrassed herself in front of everyone… in front of Ben. It was hard to swallow the memory down and smile, but she did her best as she offered a non-answer: "Work keeps me pretty busy."

Ben bobbed his head, still looking mortified. *Good. Let him feel ruffled for once, rather than me.* Allison opened her mouth, about to fire back a question at Meghan Whitfield about *her* significant others… until she remembered that— she was pretty sure—Meghan's husband had died a few years ago. Instead, she said, "So do you run this farm all by yourself?"

"Nah, I have a very capable co-owner," Meghan said. She jerked her head toward a teenage girl in the living room, who appeared to be flirting with a boy around her age. *Ah.* It was Sarah, Ben's niece, the one he'd brought to the skating rink. Allison thought the boy with her might be the same one from the rink, though it was hard to tell… kids of that age all looked the same to her now, gangly and unsure.

"That's great she helps with the chores and everything," Allison said.

"If she ever stops, she'd better have a darn good reason." Now that Meghan's attention was attracted to her daughter, she couldn't stop looking over there. "Like, a young gentleman would be a poor reason to neglect her farm duties, including as co-hostess of the annual Christmas party... will you excuse me?"

Without waiting for an answer, Ben's sister strode off in the direction of Sarah and her male friend (or suitor?). Sarah visibly gulped, and Allison couldn't help but laugh at the sight.

"I'm so sorry for Meghan prying into your personal life," Ben said hurriedly as soon as Meghan was out of earshot. "That's not... I didn't tell her to ask about that, or anything."

Allison cocked her hip. "Why *would* you have told her to ask about my relationship status?"

Ben reddened. "There'd be no reason. No reason at all. That's why I didn't."

She let him dangle a few seconds longer, then said, "Anyway, it was no problem. You... heard firsthand my luck with big-city romance, that day when I was yelling into the phone. There's no need to elaborate on that topic any more."

"Agreed," Ben responded, sounding relieved. "Can I get you some punch? Some sliced ham and, uhm, salad?"

"I can get it," she said, and she moved to the long table where the foods and beverages were arrayed in humble but homey dishes and plates. As she filled her plate, she glanced backward at Ben and saw that he was watching her. Good, he deserved to twist in the wind. She didn't enjoy mind games, but once they'd been used on her, it was only fair to employ them in return.

Well, at least the food looked pretty good here. *Tasted* more than pretty good, she amended after popping a bit of brown-sugared ham into her mouth. She washed it down with a swig of red punch, the surface of which swirled mysteriously.

Ben grabbed his own food and beverage and then joined her. "Do you see any familiar faces here?" he asked.

She scanned the crowd. "A few. A couple of them I'd have to… confirm if they are who I think they are."

"You really have been away from Holloway Green for too long," Ben said lightly. "You see that woman with the crazy hat over there, talking with the gentlemen who are twins?"

"Yep…"

"That's Mayor Beaulieu. Deadbeat in chief. I don't think that Meghan actually invited her to this party, but the mayor has a way of sniffing out parties that she deems advantageous to her."

"You don't sound like you're a big fan of the mayor," Allison observed.

Ben shook his head with surprising force. He gestured at the mayor with a piece of chicken. "She's been looking the other way while times got tough for this town. Same with the town council, or at least the councilors with the last name of Holloway. Yes, everywhere has been suffering during the bad economy, but Holloway Green didn't have to get sucked into the same fate. We needed a plan, and neither Mayor Beaulieu nor the council bothered to come up with one."

"Well, like I said the other day, maybe you should consider running for town council yourself. Or even for mayor."

He didn't answer. Allison found that she was shoveling appetizers into her mouth in a mechanical motion. They were good, when she paid attention to tasting them—what a selection!—but the action was no solution to the anxiety she was feeling. She still felt a little *off* standing here with Ben, the two of them stiff beside each other, so she tried a fresh tack of conversation.

"So how are things going at the bookstore?" she asked.

"You already asked me that," Ben said, with a slight smile. Teasing, even.

Allison flushed. *Stupid*. "What I mean is, what are the most popular books that you're moving right now? What's selling the most copies?"

Ben shrugged. "The holiday-themed stuff is really moving, of course. But there's been a surprising jump in sales for that YA book series about the talking horse. I didn't think there was any kid left in America who didn't have every book in the series by now."

"That tracks with what I know about book sales," Allison replied, laughing. "I feel like parents are buying second or third copies of the books for their kids, when there are so many other, lesser-known YA authors who are great. People can be hesitant to branch out."

Ben simply nodded in return, and Allison found she didn't want to discuss books about talking horses right now after all. But the topic of horses seemed unavoidable. "You've got a wonderful sister," she said. "And she has a beautiful home. How long has she been living here? Did she inherit this farm or start it up herself?"

He took a sip of the red punch before answering. "Meghan and her late husband operated this farm together, rehabilitating it after the previous owner left it a wreck. It had always been her husband's dream to own a horse farm; Meghan had to grow into loving it herself, but now I think she's a more hardcore farmer than even Bruce ever was. She's been teaching Sarah all the ways of the farm. But my sister has no expectation that Sarah will stick around and do this for a career. She's encouraging Sarah to apply to colleges next year and explore different interests."

"That sounds healthy," Allison said. She thought of the pressure Dad had initially put on her to work at the ski lodge like her siblings, but then pushed the negative thought away.

She smiled and said, "Did you ever have the inclination to pick up a pitchfork or a hoe yourself?"

Ben shook his head emphatically. "Trust me, I'm a fan of the great outdoors, and I support local agriculture, but I've never had any interest in mucking out stables or growing crops. I'm not a salt-of-the-earth kind of guy. I mean, I'm all for carpentry and working with my hands, as you've seen, but more on inside projects than outdoor projects."

"No, that totally makes sense," Allison said. "I guess I'm pretty much the same. Even growing up here, I never had the urge to join 4H in school, never dreamed of riding ponies or whatever. I guess there was a little city girl in me long before I actually moved to New York."

Then a thought occurred to her. "Ben, I don't see Grandpa Skip anywhere. I assumed he'd be at this party."

He frowned. "Yeah, I was surprised I didn't see him here either. I'll have to stop by his place afterward."

"You definitely should." Allison hesitated, then made a final effort to expel the emotional weight still lodged in her chest. "Hey… you're not still mad at me about the Evie thing, are you? I am so sorry to meddle like that. I should never have listened to Sam. I—I didn't mean to hurt anyone's feelings."

Ben's features softened as he looked at her, and Allison felt a flush creep through her body. To be the subject of his full attention like this, to have his bewitching eyes on him, was an intense experience indeed.

"It's all right," he said. "I realized it was all Sam's dumb idea. Ghost Boy tends to have lots of dumb ideas, as you may have noticed, so it completely tracks. I'm sorry for making it seem like I was still mad at you." He raised his glass of punch to her. "Why don't we toast to our friendship, and letting nothing get in its way? It's Christmastime. This is the season to let go of silly misunderstandings."

She happily raised her glass to clink with his, relieved to feel her guilt melt away. "Amen to that! Cheers to you, Ben Whitfield, and to Christmas. And friendship."

Then Allison realized that during their conversation, they had wandered over to the fireplace, away from the rest of Meghan's friends and family. She let out a little sigh of contentment examining the hearth, which was decked out with evergreen garlands with little red plaid bows. The sight brought a little tug of remembrance in her heart for Christmases past.

As her gaze traveled up from the fireplace to the chimney, she noticed a sprig of mistletoe was hanging from one of the farmhouse's wooden ceiling beams. Directly above their heads.

Her cheeks reddened as she saw that Ben had followed the direction of her gaze and was looking at the mistletoe as well. He gave her a small grin.

"Well, since we're paying tribute to the season," Ben said in a soft, almost gentle voice, "we ought to observe the appropriate Christmas tradition here too."

"Yes, of course," Allison said lightly, though her heart was hammering. "It's one of the most important traditions, after all. It's the reason mistletoe was invented. And to defy the tradition would just be bad luck…"

"And I don't want any bad luck right now, especially with the bookstore in such a precarious position," Ben said, nodding. "You're absolutely right."

Their eyes locked. For a moment, the world was just the two of them… the rest of the party crowd, the farmhouse, the hearth, the mistletoe itself all faded away. Allison swam through the liquid of Ben's gaze. Then he closed his eyes, and she closed her eyes too. They leaned toward each other, Allison's quailing heart still racing.

Then a rough shout rang out from the foyer, shattering

the moment: "Ho! Ho! Ho! A tremendously merry Christmas to all of you children, young and old!"

A Santa Claus in a bright, artificially red suit had burst through the door while Allison's attention was elsewhere. He had a big bag slung over his shoulder, and carried a boombox under his other arm. He thrust his belly out to the crowd and said, "Let's get this party started for real! I need all you kids to call out, *Go, Santa, Go!*"

He switched on the boombox and the Chipmunks Christmas song began to play. Santa put his boombox and voluminous bag on the floor and gyrated to the music. Every child in attendance squealed in delight, except for Sarah, who was of course too old and too cool for that. Who was that Santa, Allison wondered. Judging by the booming voice, probably Tony Dietrich, owner of Antonio's Ristorante.

The spell between them long since broken, Allison and Ben looked at each other; she noticed he was blinking in apparent confusion. He jerked away from her and straightened up, as if he had been out of his mind when proposing the mistletoe kiss. He walked toward the crowd, and Allison quickly followed.

Yes, she thought in a rush of jumbled thoughts, *Let's cheer on Santa. Maybe he needs some help handing out gifts.*

She and Ben did join the effort to distribute the presents to the kids when Santa's silly dance was over, but there was no way she could release her thoughts completely from what had just happened—or rather, what had *almost* happened. *Was that a bluff? Was one of us supposed to break away at the last second, like a game of Mistletoe Chicken? Or was... that... actually going to happen?*

She wasn't ready. An image of Peter reared up in her head like the Ghost of Christmas Jerkface. Ben was so nice, so handsome, so funny and strong and determined, but...

Allison felt a bolt of fear shoot through her chest. She

turned to Ben and said, "Hey, I'm not feeling that well. Too many snacks, I think—do you mind if we take off in a few minutes?"

"Sure, yeah, that's fine," he rushed to agree with her, far too quickly. She noted the redness in his cheeks, and she felt obscurely guilty.

"I'm so sorry," she said. "I don't mean to take you away from your family so soon. You should come back to the party after dropping me off. Or, no, listen to how selfish I'm being. I could just find another ride. I could call a rideshare. I could do that, right? I heard Wally Tucker's running a rideshare in this town."

But his mouth set in a firm line and he said, "Wally's probably not gonna be running his rides with the snow so persistent tonight. And you wouldn't want to put him in danger anyway, he's got that dumb little Prius that's no match for a few inches of snow. My truck can handle it with no problem. Let me take you."

CHAPTER 14

*B*en attempted to focus on the road ahead through the driving snow, though he was having plenty of trouble. He repeatedly resisted the urge to look over at the beautiful woman beside him, repeatedly reliving the *moment* between them.

He couldn't believe they had almost kissed. He couldn't believe that he had suggested it; the mistletoe was a thin excuse for a romantic advance indeed, and everyone knew it. What was wrong with him? Clearly she thought that he was a creep, since she'd so rapidly asked for him to take her home. He'd obliged her in a hurry, feeling the sting of embarrassment and shame.

He fumbled for the radio—maybe it'd do the job of drowning out his thoughts. For once he couldn't find any Christmas music; the snow was messing with the signal. He settled on a droning public radio voice, but that didn't help.

You moved too fast. And weren't you supposed to learn a lesson from the Evie setup thing, you dope?!

Yes, he was supposed to recognize it as a sign: that she couldn't be interested in Ben herself, if she was so eager to

148

set him up with someone else. Even if it had been Sam's idea. *No, this was a dumb trap that I first set for myself, then stepped right into.* He wasn't smart enough to act like a full-grown adult, much less run a bookstore.

When he pulled up in front of the O'Briens' fine home, Allison fairly leapt out of her seat and out of the car, only then ducking her head back in as she remembered to thank him and say goodbye. He let her off with a brusque single word of farewell, knowing that however awkward he felt, this must be twice as awkward for her—though it still pained him to watch her stumble through the new-fallen snow on her parents' walk in her haste to get to the house and away from him.

Really, Ben was a jerk for trying to kiss her so soon after her messy breakup with her boyfriend from New York. He shouldn't have seen her breakup as his "chance," but instead as a signal to just let her relax and heal for a while. She needed a friend right now, not some creepy mistletoe kisser man.

It was just as well that he'd left the party early. His worry about Grandpa Skip now returned to him afresh. He had to brave the driving snow to go over to his grandfather's house and check on him. He'd failed over and over again to get the old man to open up about his feelings, but Ben had to try one more time. He owed it to Grandpa Skip.

He saw lights on in the windows of his grandfather's house; clearly the old man was still awake. Ben knocked on the door. He heard a faint, hoarse holler, and less than a minute later, the door opened.

Grandpa Skip looked fine physically, standing tall and sturdy as ever. But his expression was melancholy, and it didn't change much at the sight of his grandson. In fact, he looked a little annoyed. "Mr. Ben," he said. "Please come in."

Ben walked into the modest living room, shucking off his

coat and gloves and hanging them up. As usual, his grandparents' house stirred up a ton of memories with a force that was overpowering. He could almost see his grandmother sitting in the corner of the room, in her favorite flower-patterned chair. *It must be like this for Grandpa Skip every day.* The thought saddened him.

"Meghan was disappointed that you didn't come to the party," he said. "I was too. I thought you were going to ride over with your neighbor." He realized he was framing his sentiment as a guilt trip, but it was still better than having the old man think that he was the subject of everyone's worry—and pity. That had been the fear that Grandpa Skip had expressed, after all.

"Well, I appreciate the invite," Grandpa Skip said, "but I didn't feel up to it… being around all those people, having to make conversation with them, pretend to care about their responses. When you're my age, you'll understand why parties have a limited appeal."

"I know holidays are tough, and you must be thinking about Grandma," Ben said. "But it might be easier for you if you spend more time with family—rather than being alone in this house with your memories of her."

"Oh, do you think that's what I do all day?" Grandpa Skip said, with a touch of indignation. But also, Ben was surprised to see, with an impish gleam in his eyes. "I'll have you know, you interrupted me in the middle of working on my project."

There it was again. The "project." "All right, this time I have to insist you tell me what it is."

"Oh, fine, you insolent little snot," his grandfather said, with genuine good humor. "Why don't you come with me into the dining room and I'll show you?"

He followed his grandfather into the living room, where he was shocked at the sight of a magnificent model of a cog railway train on a mountain, covering the vast surface of the table.

He'd thought Grandpa Skip had abandoned his model train hobby long ago. Now, here was a model he'd never seen before. The cog railway ran more steeply than a regular train, with a bright red passenger car attached to the locomotive. It must be the one that ran up nearby Mount Washington. There was a town nestled at the foot of the mountain, however, which was a fiction. He peered at the little buildings: the proud tower of a town hall, a scattering of shops around a town square, a green park framed by historic houses...

"This is Holloway Green," he murmured. "I even see The Old Bookshop!"

"That's right."

"How—how did you..." he stammered. He was at a loss for words, but he still kept groping for them. "When did you..."

"It's been a while," Grandpa Skip said. "Months. Pretty much since I hung up my hat at the bookstore, in fact. And I've been working on this for *you*."

"For *me*? Why?"

Grandpa Skip drew his bushy white eyebrows together. "Because I love you. And I'm proud of you—so proud of you."

Ben felt a lump rising in his throat as his grandfather continued: "But remember, I've been working on this since *before* you took on this bookstore challenge. I'm proud of you whether you succeed or fail to meet the goal by Christmas. I hope you know that."

"I don't... know what to say," Ben whispered. "Except for the fact that—Meghan is going to be *really* jealous."

"Pah. Trains are boy stuff." Grandpa Skip grinned. "I suppose you did catch me in a lie about not going to the party. The truth is, I've been running behind schedule on making my finishing touches to this monster. I needed to put in some extra hours tonight, and tomorrow too, to have this ready to give to you on Christmas. But... now you've gone and come over here and spoiled the surprise. You've only got yourself to blame for that."

Ben blinked back tears. "I'm, I'm... wow. That's okay, Grandpa Skip. This means so much to me."

Grandpa Skip chuckled. "Now I do miss Helen power-fully at this time of year, you're right about that. But projects like this train model do help. Especially when there's a dead-line. Now, you're still gonna have to give me until Christmas to finish up—"

"Oh, you don't have to rush. And I mean, I could help you."

"No, sir, this is something I'm doing on my own. And I *do* want to have it finished by Christmas, and not just for your sake. The only string I'm attaching to this gift is that you have to display it prominently in the bookstore." Grandpa Skip squared his shoulders with obvious pride. "This train model could give the bookstore real character."

"That it certainly would," Ben said with sincerity. As he circled the mountain, he was thinking that people would come to visit the bookstore *just* to see this impressive model. He also loved the thought of Grandpa Skip's own character given pride of place in the bookstore. "This is amazing, Grandpa. I... am surprised, though, that you added Holloway Green to a model of the Mount Wash-ington Cog Railway. You're not usually one for artistic license."

"Maybe I'm trying be a little more flexible in my old age."

Ben feigned a shocked look. "It's a Christmas miracle!"

"Don't pretend you don't love it," Grandpa Skip said. "Now, do you mind if I give you a little talking to, on this eve before Christmas Eve?" He had a twinkle in his eye.

"About what?" Ben replied. His guard went up automatically.

"You've been throwing yourself into the bookstore," his grandfather said, "just as you threw so much of yourself into your humanitarian work. Your whole self, even. Your work ethic, Mr. Ben, that's something I've always admired about you. But you might be neglecting one important detail."

"And what's that?" Ben asked, bracing for criticism of the bookstore. He thought he'd paid attention to every vital detail of running the business. But, of course, he was a neophyte to the field, and he still had so much to learn...

"I'm talking about love," Grandpa Skip said. "One of the most important parts of this Christmas season."

"Oh," Ben said. This was... certainly an interesting moment to bring the subject up, just a short time after he had almost kissed Allison and then driven her away from him. "That's not—"

"I am very proud of what I built in the bookstore," Grandpa Skip rolled on. "But it would've meant *nothing* to me if I didn't have Helen by my side the whole time. Perhaps that's why I felt like I could let the bookstore go this year. Without her, it's just not the same. Boy, I don't want you to lose yourself in the work so much that you never make the time to find your own Helen."

"Believe me, I've been setting time aside to have my own romantic misadventures," Ben said ruefully. Then he blurted, without meaning to, the whole story: "I almost kissed Allison tonight. Under the mistletoe, at Meghan's party. I don't know what I was thinking... she'd just had a painful breakup with her boyfriend in New York, and I should've given her space. We didn't end up kissing. Tony showed up at the party in his Santa suit right then, and Allison and I both pulled back. She seemed pretty eager to go home after that."

Grandpa Skip folded his arms and looked at Ben. "And?"

"And that's it. I should've just left her alone."

"And you're going to give up just like that?" Grandpa Skip asked incredulously. "That doesn't sound like you. Are you sure she didn't want you to kiss her?"

"Pretty sure, since she wanted to go home so quickly."

"But you don't *know*. Maybe she didn't want to kiss in front of 'Santa.'" Grandpa Skip shook his head. "You can't assume what's going on in her head. Come on, Mr. Ben! You should ask her out on a real date, and see what happens. Not a party, but something where it's just the two of you."

"I don't know. It's Christmas, and she's got enough on her mind."

"Like heck. Listen, you still got time. Ask her out to dinner at Antonio's. She says no, then you have your answer."

Ben bit his lip and shook his head. "Grandpa Skip, it's... not that simple. She doesn't even live here anymore."

"Then if she rejects you, you can blame it on the distance," Grandpa Skip said philosophically. "Worst case, she laughs in your face and it'll be a funny story she can tell her lady friends afterward. The time that cheeky slob Ben Whitfield *dared* to ask her out."

He found himself smiling. "Ah, c'mon. She would never do that."

"There you go. Allison's too classy a lady to make you feel bad. Nothing to worry about. Listen, you're a wonderful young man, and if she isn't the one for you, you'll certainly find someone else. You'll never know until you take action."

But I don't want someone else, he found himself thinking automatically. He desperately wanted to bring this particular topic to a close, so he said, "You're right, Grandpa Skip. I've got nothing to lose by asking her."

Then he changed the subject. "So are you gonna show me this this train line in action or what? I want to see how it operates."

The old man pushed his glasses up his nose. "All right, although again, you're spoiling your Christmas surprise. But if you insist, I guess you're already here and so we might as well make the most of it." He shuffled toward the kitchen. "Let me make some hot chocolate for you and then we can run this thing around the track together."

"I'll help, Grandpa. You have any marshmallows?"

Later, when Ben left his grandfather's house and returned to his apartment, he found himself in a much better mood than he would've anticipated for himself earlier tonight. For that, he was grateful. The mood lasted through the morning; he woke the next day with a renewed sense of purpose, going into the bookstore early to work the last shift before he'd close down the shop in mid-afternoon to observe Christmas Eve.

Ben had been promoting the heck out of the holiday hours, in his last couple of social media posts and e-mail messages introducing a sense of urgency to the bookstore's customers: *come on in and make your final gift purchases before we close up at three!*

It was funny, though, how his mindset shifted throughout the day, from sunny resistance to Grandpa Skip's old-fashioned advice to a point where they actually began to resonate with him. Maybe Ben *had* been acting like a coward.

After all, it was easy to rely on the safest interpretation of what happened last night, that Allison had been somehow repelled by the fact of them almost kissing. Maybe Allison *had* really wanted to kiss, and was so disappointed when they didn't, that that was why she said she just wanted to go home.

He *hadn't* imagined that trace of light in her eyes. She had agreed to observe the "holiday tradition" with him, now that he thought back to her exact words. He *hadn't* acted like a creep. Right?

Yes, it's Christmastime, he thought to himself as he wrapped up a customer's book in bright, festive paper. He fumbled tying the bow as he thought of Allison's soft features. Yes, it was time to open his heart—what else was the holiday season for, as Grandpa had said? His heart had been shut for too long, trying to protect himself from hurt and abandonment. What did he really have to lose, opening it to Allison?

Maybe it was the relentless Christmas music he was playing in the store that got to him, seeping into his brain, but a daft idea began to form there.

CHAPTER 15

*C*hristmas Eve was far less blustery and snowy than the previous night, though a light fall of white still lent atmosphere outside the frosted windows of the family room. Allison was with her family on Christmas Eve, and though she chatted merrily with them and was having a great time, her heart was elsewhere. She kept thinking about that almost kiss. What would it have been like to have Ben's lips on hers? And why did they stop? Was it really Santa's fault?

Or was it her hesitation?

She still wasn't sure. Her heart was in far more turmoil than she preferred. She didn't consider herself a wishy-washy person, but the answer to what, exactly, to do now was far from clear. What Peter did to her—the scars had barely healed, and they'd just been ripped open again the other day.

Yes, Ben was a great guy. An amazing guy, even. But it was surely too soon to jump into something else.

And Ben might not even have meant the kiss thing as more than a gesture of friendship either. Maybe he'd been about to kiss her on the cheek, which would have been sweet and seasonally appropriate. Not to mention platonic. If that were the case, he'd probably written her off as a total mess by now.

She forced her attention back to the O'Brien family's soothing scene of domestic peace, if marred by the occasional squabble. The five of them were gathered in the family room by the big Christmas tree. Dad's attention seemed elsewhere, as usual—he was probably worrying about the ski lodge—but Mom was talking with Christine about their last-minute shopping adventures, reliving some of the direr perils they'd encountered downtown in the holiday rush.

Meanwhile, Sam was jabbing at Allison with insinuations about her attending the Christmas party with Ben. "Guy asks you to his sister's holiday party, that usually only means one thing."

"There's nothing there," she said firmly, "and that's all there is to it. So let's just talk about something else."

"Like how you ate my slice of bûche de noël the other night? Don't think I didn't notice."

"You deserved it," Allison said. "End of topic. Now I want to hear more about ghosts. You mentioned that gig you got investigating the courthouse in Ossipee, but what about here in Holloway Green? What's the most haunted place in town?"

Her brother gave her an enigmatic smile. "Hard to narrow down. Holloway Green's got such an interesting history. All the artists that used to live here—their creative energy lingers. Takes on a spirit of its own, sometimes. One guy, a freed slave, came north to town, lived where the Winter Rose B&B is now, and produced the most amazing paintings... or so they say, anyway, because none of them exist anymore. Local bigot brigade torched his entire body of work one night. Artist himself only narrowly escaped, and he was never the same after. Some guests at the bed and breakfast swear they've seen his ghost searching for his lost paintings… or sometimes creating new ones…"

Allison made spooky gestures with her fingers. "Sounds like a story Celia Drake concocted to drum up business at her B&B."

"It's true, I swear," Sam said. "Anyway, you reminded me of a new Christmas Eve tradition I'd love to establish with you guys." He raised his voice to address the entire family. "What do you guys think about telling ghost stories tonight? People used to do that all the time on Christmas Eve; I think they still do in Britain. Like, that scary ghost stories line in the 'It's the Most Wonderful Time of the Year' song?"

"Well, sure," Dad said, with a faint grimace, "but I don't know any. Do you girls?"

Christine rolled her eyes. Allison was momentarily at a loss. She knew she must have heard or read a thousand ghost stories in her lifetime, but none of them came to mind. Maybe she could steal a ghostly legend about the New York Public Library from the internet or something. "I'm gonna need a few minutes to come up with one," she said. "But Sam, I assume that you have one already. To kick us off."

"Of course," Sam said. "I've got the perfect one for this occasion. But first we have to dim the lights, to create the right atmosphere. Christine, can you get the lights?"

"How about you get the lights?" Christine grumbled. But she got up anyway and flicked the switches. Now the only illumination in the room was from the crackling fire and the multicolored lights of the Christmas tree.

"So," Sam said, "this is an old story, and it does take place around Christmastime, but I should warn you: it's pretty scary."

"Get on with it, Edgar Allan," Christine put in.

"It's a legend that takes place right here in Holloway Green," Sam continued, unperturbed. "It dates back to the time of the Civil War. A young Union soldier got married just before he went off to war, which of course is never a great idea. His bride waited for him here in town as he went south to fight in the Battle of Gettysburg.

"Sadly for him, he would not return alive from the battle. The bride had a lucky rabbit's foot that her husband had given her just before leaving. He had said, 'Don't worry about me; just as long as you hold onto that, I'll be able to come back home to you.' When the terrible news arrived via telegram, it seemed frankly unfair to her that his words had turned out to be a lie. Late one night, by the hearth in her bedroom—with a fire going *just like* the one we have right now—the young widow took the rabbit's foot in her hands and wished upon it to fulfill the promise her soldier love had made to her. She wished that her husband would come back to her, would return from Gettysburg at that very moment, no matter what the words on some telegram had told her. She wished hard on that lucky rabbit's foot, harder than she had ever wished for anything in her life.

"And then she heard it. A knock on the door downstairs. A slow, deliberate knock. The most intense thrill ran through the young widow. He was back—he was really back! As she headed down the stairs, however, a troubling thought occurred to her. She had perhaps not been specific enough in her wish for him to return to her... shouldn't she have said, 'Return alive and in one piece, just like you were when you left?' What if she opened the door and he was all bloody, with the head wound that he had received in Gettysburg? Did she really want him back like *that*?

"There is a slow knock on the door again. Frozen on the stairs, she called out in a shrill voice, 'Who is it?!'

"No voice answered her. Only the knock, sounding again. From where she was standing, she could see through the window near the door that there was a shadowy figure there, but she couldn't tell its form, whether it was male or female, living or dead. Her heart beat so fast she thought she was about to keel over and die herself. The widow was frantic, trying to think about what to do next. She looked down at the rabbit's foot in her hands and fervently wished for the visitor to go away. She wished just as hard as she'd wished for her husband to come back.

"But it was no use. She heard a knock again.

"In a final act of desperation, she flew back up the stairs and threw the 'lucky' rabbit's foot into the into the dying flames of her bedroom hearth. She stood stock still, listening. There were no more knocks. Summoning the last of her courage, she went to the front door and opened it. There was nothing there."

A moment of silence greeted the end of Sam's story. Then Allison said, "You totally ripped off The Monkey's—"

That was when a knock sounded—on *their* front door. Everyone jumped up from their seats, Christine letting out a little yelp, Mom gripping Dad by his bicep, Allison reaching for a fireplace poker. Even Sam looked ash-white.

There was another knock, and a muffled voice said, "Hello? Anyone in there?"

The voice was unmistakably that of a human with a pulse. Allison relaxed, though she still held onto the poker. "Great timing, Sam," she said. "You really got us. So which one of your friends is out there?"

Sam looked at her in a panic. "I didn't set this up, I swear! *It could be a ghost,* so don't answer the door!"

"Nonsense," Mom said, though her voice quavered as she called out, "Who is it?"

There was no answer—though to be fair, Mom hadn't called out very loudly.

"Give me that thing, sweetheart," Dad said, holding out his hand for the fireplace poker. Allison surrendered the poker with some reluctance, and Dad brandished it as he approached the front door. Allison quickly followed him; she was close behind him when he seized the doorknob and yanked the door open to reveal their evening visitor.

She was shocked to see Peter standing there in the doorway.

Her ex-boyfriend looked weirdly out of place here on a rural winter night—incongruous, as if a small piece of Manhattan had been chiseled away and deposited on their doorstep. He was wearing a thousand-dollar slim-fitting coat that looked unsuited to any temperature below forty degrees. Peter's ungloved hands clutched a bouquet of distressed-looking roses. He gave her an uncertain smile.

"Hi, Allison," he said.

"Who the heck are you?" Dad said.

"I'm Allison's boyfriend," Peter said. "I've come to ask her if she'll take me back."

The absolute nerve! She goggled at him, unable to even speak in that moment. It was frankly ludicrous that Peter had traveled all the way up here from New York... to just show up at her family's doorstep unannounced, and expect her to take him back after the way he'd treated her? She kept running through outraged retorts in her head, tripping up because she couldn't decide on the right one.

"Is this true?" Dad said, squinting at her. She noted that he kept his body between his daughter and the intruder; the rush of gratitude that flowed through her helped her collect her thoughts.

She sighed, then turned to Peter. "Dude, you are not my boyfriend. You lost that privilege when you cheated on me."

By now the rest of the family had crowded behind her and Dad. Peter gave them a frightened look, as if he suddenly realized he was outnumbered, but then cleared his throat and said, in a slightly unnatural tone, "Please, just hear me out.

I've come a long way and I've been doing a lot of thinking. Will you please just give me five minutes, Allison?"

Dad pushed the tip of the fireplace poker against Peter's chest. Gently, but the point was unmistakable. "You've got five *seconds*—to get the heck out of here. How dare you? On Christmas Eve?!"

But Mom put a hand on Dad's shoulder. "Dear—Allie— maybe she should give him his five minutes, *because* it's Christmas Eve. The man is standing there shivering in the cold after traveling all the way from New York City. Allison, will you let him step into the foyer, at least, for those five minutes only?"

Allison turned to Mom, taken aback. How could her mother be taking the side of this stranger to her, this person that she'd clearly told her mother had hurt her so badly? "Mom—"

"Closure," Mom said then, enunciating the word distinctly. "That's what you need, isn't it?"

It was like a magic word, clarifying Allison's thoughts. She remembered the discussion with her mother the other day about *closure.* And she realized Mom had a point. If this could be an opportunity to banish Peter like a demon from her thoughts, what was the harm in taking it? They did outnumber Peter, after all.

"All right," Allison said. "I can't believe I'm saying this, but come in, Peter. Mom's right... I do need closure. So, use your five minutes wisely, Peter." Then, she added, "Grovel before me."

Her sister let out a little chuckle, quickly stifled. Allison quirked a brow at her, then motioned for the whole family to step back, to allow her ex-boyfriend room to occupy the foyer along with them.

Peter's face lit up with sudden hope as he came in, heedlessly dripping melting flakes of snow onto the wooden floor. His eyes flicked to the upper left, as if he were pulling his speech from memory. Then he put on a smooth smile that Allison was all too familiar with, signaling a charm offensive.

"All right, so here's the thing," he said. "I know I was fooling around with those other women, and that's a bad thing. No question about it. But the truth is, I was thinking about you the whole time, even when I was with them. How your hair shines in the reflected light from the office buildings on Park Avenue. The way that you eat your paninis from the takeout stand on West 44th Street..."

She realized Peter was attempting to woo her with lines that he'd paraphrased from a romantic comedy movie, if not stolen outright. She interrupted his monologue. "Hey. You're going to have to do better than that. Do you actually feel any remorse for lying to me and cheating on me?

Peter nodded his head in a burst of enthusiasm. "*Absolutely.* I have been wracked with guilt for weeks now. Every day I'm obsessed with how guilty I feel—it's such an unpleasant feeling. Every day I say to myself, 'I really hate that Allison is mad at me.'"

"That's not really what guilt is," Christine observed.

But Allison held up her hand, suppressing a smirk. She said, "Please, continue, Peter."

Peter, oblivious to the fact that his audience could see right through him, continued. "I really hate that I wake up in the morning and I have to feel bad," he said. "I hate that Julie and Kim broke up with me and found other guys. But most of all, I hate that I can't stop thinking about you, because you're just so beautiful, Allison."

"Is that so?" Allison said in a neutral tone. She exchanged a quick look with her mother, who nodded, as if to say, *Go on, you know what to do.* "So, I'm beautiful. What are some other great qualities about me?"

"Well," Peter said, "you are… gorgeous. And you look great next to me when we're out in the City. And you're very good-looking, every part of you. I like your eyes. And your hair. And your body, it—"

"That's enough on *that* subject," Dad broke in. His voice was unexpectedly gentle as he asked, "What do you like about my daughter's personality, young man?"

"Oh, so many things," Peter said, though he was visibly struggling with the question. "I like that she's smart. I like that she laughs at the jokes that I make. I like that she never gets lost on the subway or takes the wrong train, even when they're running express trains…"

"I'm sorry, I can't listen to any more of this," Sam said, evidently missing the point of the game. "This is just pathetic."

Peter turned toward him angrily. "And who are *you*—the new boyfriend?"

"This is my brother Sam," Allison said. "I mentioned to you that I have a younger brother, many times."

"Oh," Peter said. His trademark smooth smile returned. "I knew that. I was just joking with you."

No one seemed convinced, but Peter continued on anyway. "I like your personality because I like the way you give me compliments. And—"

He turned, startled, as there was another knock at the door.

"Are you *sure* you didn't set all this up?" Allison asked Sam, whirling on him. "That's one too many knocks for one night—now is *this* one of your buddies showing up just to bolster your stupid ghost story?"

"No," Sam said, holding up his hands to fend her off, "I swear. I'm not that smart. Really. This is just a weird—"

The new arrival knocked again. And then the door opened a crack and a tentative face peeked through.

CHAPTER 16

The rush of certainty that Ben had experienced while he was working at the bookstore evaporated as he drove his car through the sleepy Christmas Eve of Holloway Green, heading to where Allison's parents lived at the base of Jackpine Mountain.

It had *seemed* like such a good idea amid the fever of his initial enthusiasm. So romantic. Now his little plan lost its sheen, the more he thought about it: showing up at a woman's house on Christmas Eve to ask her out? What if his gesture was interpreted as... you know... psychotic? Lonely and desperate?

Ben glanced down at the box of holiday chocolates on the front seat next to him. It looked pathetic to him now. Yes, desperate was a good word for it.

Then he remembered the wisdom of Grandpa Skip. The way he could almost see his grandmother sitting in her armchair in his grandparents' house. Wasn't it worth looking foolish, even pathetic, if he had a chance to be with Allison? He couldn't just dodge all opportunities for intimacy and love for the rest of his life.

So he forced his doubts aside and kept going. The plan was simple. Say hi and Merry Christmas. Present the chocolates. Ask her on a real date. Like Grandpa Skip said, the worst that could happen would be that she'd laugh about him with her friends later. And if that was the case—which he highly doubted it would be—then they weren't meant to be together anyway.

He pulled up in front of the O'Brien house, behind an unfamiliar car parked on the street, a fancy ride with rental plates. He took a deep breath and stepped out of the car. Whatever happened, Ben was determined not to embarrass Allison in front of her family. He would simply take her aside and quietly ask her out. That was the sensible way to do it. Well, first give her the chocolates, then ask her out. Wait— the chocolates.

He went back to the car and retrieved the box from the front seat, then navigated the icy front walk to the front door. He knocked, then realized he could hear raised voices in conversation very close by, almost as if they were right on the other side of the door. They paused briefly at the knock and then continued. Maybe nobody had actually heard him. He knocked again and then, wincing, opened the O'Briens' door just a crack.

He peered in and said, "Hello? I'm so sorry to interrupt on Christmas Eve. I just—"

Then he froze. The entire O'Brien family was gathered in the foyer for some reason, looking tensely at him. A tall, skinny, handsome man stood with him, wearing an expensive coat and looking out of place. That couldn't be…

Was that the boyfriend from New York?

Oh good God, he thought. *They made up.*

As if sensing his cue, the stranger stepped forward and stuck his hand out. "Hi, I'm Peter," he said. "I'm Allison's boyfriend. And you are?"

Ben made no move to accept the handshake. His blood seemed to be freezing in its veins. He looked from this Peter to Allison, and then said, "I'm... in the wrong house, I think."

"Hey, Ben—" Allison started to say.

"It's fine," Ben said, unable to work through the jumble of crushing thoughts in his head, "Merry Christmas! To all a good night!"

He turned his back on all of them and stumbled as he stepped off the front stoop. He wasn't running—he could preserve his dignity enough to at least avoid running—but he walked at a swift pace back down the front walk. A very swift pace.

Halfway to his car, his feet betrayed him. The ground was no longer solid beneath his feet, no longer there at all. The dark sky whirled above Ben and he crashed down on the ice coating the walk. He let out a little cry as his limbs tangled. The box of chocolates went flying, breaking open and scattering truffles, some of which came to rest on the ice, while the others disappeared into the white of the lawn. He looked behind him and saw multiple O'Briens crowding in the doorway, their concern apparent on their faces.

Allison called out, "Ben!"

"I'm OK," Ben said gallantly, picking himself up and wincing at the slight twinge in his right leg. "I'm fine, don't worry about me!"

He limped to his car. He heard Allison calling out to him to wait, but he didn't look back—he couldn't look back. Ben turned the key in the ignition; his engine coughed, and for one horrible instant he was sure the car would betray him too, would leave him at the mercy of Allison and her lover and her entire family. Their pity would be palpable.

But, no, thankfully, after another hiccup, the car came to life, and Ben was able to make his escape.

At least you tried, Grandpa Skip's voice said in his head, now sounding mocking rather than helpful.

Yeah, whatever. Ben couldn't believe that Allison had invited the boyfriend up for Christmas after all. How could she take him back after he'd hurt her so much? She deserved so much better than that. But, he reminded himself, Allison was a grownup; she could make her own decisions.

He had to respect her decisions, even if they seemed all wrong to him.

Ben lost focus for a while, numbed by disappointment and sadness and hypnotized by the light snow swirling out of the darkness, until he reached the downtown area. He parked and looked up at the window of his apartment, above the store. He realized, with a pang, *I don't think I can bear being up there. Alone on Christmas Eve.* No, the thought was unbearable, after what he'd seen at the O'Briens' house, and how he'd embarrassed himself.

What am I gonna do? Where am I going to go?

Then, inspiration struck him. He looked down the street, to where The Old Bookshop awaited, and marched down the sidewalk, his leg still complaining from time to time. He fumbled the keys to the bookstore from his pocket and opened the door, then switched the sign to OPEN and flipped switches until the bookstore was flooded with illumination, a weird oasis of light in the middle of the dark, slumbering downtown.

It was time for The Old Bookshop to have a *special,* unexpected, really-last-minute Christmas Eve sale. Ten percent off anything and everything! The sale and the hours of operation would run through the night, guided by Ben's steady hand. The people of Holloway Green would be so surprised and delighted by the sudden sale, they would *have* to wander into the bookstore and buy some books.

Ben smiled, feeling better for the first time since he'd fled from the O'Briens' house. Purpose! Distraction!

He sat down at the computer at the front register and blasted out an e-mail about this super surprise holiday sale happening *right now*—come one, come all! He posted about it on social media as well, along with a picture of himself in a Santa hat, holding loads of books in his arms.

This could be an annual tradition, if his future Christmas Eves were going to be lonely too...

He grimaced at that thought. And then, he waited.

Ben waited a long time. He stared at the ceramic Christmas tree on the counter, its little lights dark. The long hours of the night blurred together. He made some coffee. The street was so dark, it could have been a window into the void, as the occasional headlights of passing cars dwindled into a rarity. Then, an elderly lady in a bright green coat wandered in, as if she were an elf straight from Santa's workshop, come to cast her blessing on Ben's crazy idea.

She hesitantly approached Ben. "Are you truly open tonight? I just saw the e-mail that your store sent out."

"Yes, we are," Ben said proudly, straightening up and slapping his Santa hat back on his head. He gave her a grin. "Open all night for your last-minute Christmas needs. And ten percent off everything! What can I help you with, my friend?"

The old lady peered at him for a moment. Then she said, "That's just sad." She zipped her coat up tighter and left the store.

Ben stared after her, perplexed. "It's not sad," he said aloud, though she was already gone. "It's a clever sales strategy! What about those really-last-minute shoppers?!"

Silence answered him. More hours stretched and shrank. A few minutes after eleven, another "customer" stopped by the bookstore: a man reeking of cheap beer, who asked if he could get a two for one deal on books, and then angrily stomped out when Ben declined the possibility. And that was it. The clock first approached, then passed midnight; it was Christmas proper.

"Well," Ben said to himself, "we've still got a good number of hours left in this special Christmas sale. We're in it for the long haul, aren't we?"

And he got up from his stool to make himself a pot of fresh coffee.

CHAPTER 17

"*W*ell," Dad said, "this has been an extremely awkward and unpredictable Christmas Eve. But you need to leave now, young man. I don't care how far you came tonight."

Peter's eyes widened. "But I wasn't finished talking about all of Allison's great qualities! I wasn't finished making my case!"

"Oh, you made your case," Allison said, giving him a pleasant smile. "And now you really do need to leave. Now, there's a lovely bed and breakfast in town, but I doubt Celia will still be awake. There's also a budget motel by the highway. They'll definitely be open."

Peter gave her a last, longing look, as if he were confused about how his plan to win her back could have ever gone wrong. And then he headed down the front walk, his shoulders slumping in defeat, and very nearly took a fall on the same icy patch that had done Ben in. Allison stopped herself from laughing, but only until she closed the door. Then she let it all out.

"Oh, man, I'm sorry, everyone," she said between bursts of laughter, doubling over. "That was truly terrible."

"No, dear, that was necessary," Mom said. "Don't you feel closure now?"

Allison gave her a hug, suddenly overcome with love for her family. "You know what," she said, her heart rising, "I do. That was A-plus closure right there."

And it was true. For the first time, she actually felt good about her relationship with Peter coming to an end. Why had she ever even cared about him? She had dodged a bullet. Peter clearly never really cared about *her* until his paramours dumped him, and even then he couldn't express why he liked her other than her being attractive and laughing at his jokes.

But you know who does care about you? she thought to herself. *Perhaps the second gentleman to knock on the door on Christmas Eve...*

She was pretty sure Ben didn't come to her door with an agenda, unlike Peter. Just chocolates that had been sadly lost to the ice and snow.

As if reading her sister's mind, Christine said, "Why did Ben Whitfield leave in such a hurry? Maybe you should give him a call and make sure he's okay. That was a pretty nasty fall he took…"

"Yeah, you're right," Allison said. She could get some clarity on why he'd come by, too, if there was a reason beyond being a nice guy and delivering Christmas chocolates.

Ben didn't answer the phone. She sent him a text, but that also went unanswered, at least in the moment. Allison owed it to her family to get back to celebrating Christmas Eve with them after all these distractions, so she rejoined them in the family room.

"Hey, guys, can I get anyone some egg nog?" she asked.

Sam raised his hand. "Please."

"Only if you promise no more ghost stories," she said, giving him a shrewd look.

He shrugged. "All right, agreed. Didn't know it was gonna be such a big deal…"

The rest of the evening passed without further interruption. They settled into watching some classic Christmas movies on TV. Allison kept her ear cocked for the telltale chime of a text or a ring from her phone… nothing. If whatever Ben had to say was urgent enough to stop by on Christmas Eve, why didn't he get back in touch with her?

Clearly the sight of Peter had thrown him off. Surely Ben hadn't thought Allison was getting back together with *him*. Even if he did, why would that be cause for him to be upset?

Because he likes you, dummy.

But that was silly! He couldn't *really* think she would get together with someone as awful as Peter. Although… Ben didn't know anything about what Peter had done to her, because she'd intentionally kept that information from him. It was just so embarrassing.

Mom and Dad dropped off to sleep, and both Christine and Sam retired for the evening soon after. Allison put on her pajamas and got ready for bed, then climbed in. She found that she couldn't sleep, however; not because she was excited for Santa to come, but because she kept picturing the look on Ben's face as soon as he caught sight of Peter, there with Allison and her family. So crestfallen. So disappointed.

She had turned off her e-mail and social media on her phone for Christmas Eve, not wanting anything to distract her from crucial family time, but now she flipped them back on. She was surprised to see a message from The Old Bookshop with a "special announcement": an all-night Christmas Eve sale.

Ben hadn't mentioned anything about that before, but it had to be his idea; she couldn't imagine Grandpa Skip himself staying up the whole night. That was... a weird thing to do on Christmas. No one would show up to a sale in the middle of the night, or at least not in this town. Was Ben okay? Had he hit his head or something when he fell on the ice?

It'd stopped snowing out a while ago. Everyone else was asleep; it was well after midnight. Likely no one would miss Allison if she popped out for a quick drive, if she were quiet about it. She could drive down to the bookstore and have a quick chat with Ben, make sure everything was all right with him.

She put on her warm, thick coat over her pajamas and got in the car and drove downtown. The bookstore was not exactly swarmed with customers; there was no one else parked on the street except for Ben's car down the block.

Shivering, Allison blew on her hands for warmth as she approached the bookstore. The door was open; the place was lit up like Rockefeller Center, and it was indeed open for business. But when she walked in, she found the bookstore manager sound asleep at the counter, his head on the desk. The ceramic tree next to him wasn't lit up; that was a bad sign.

She hesitated, wondering if she should approach him and wake him up. Ultimately, she decided to let him sleep; he could probably use the extra winks. She scribbled a little note and tucked it under one of the heavy books on the foyer display, sticking out enough for him to notice it when he awoke. As she headed back out, she locked the front door, so nobody could come in and rob the place while Ben was sleeping.

Allison returned home on the silent streets and crept back upstairs undetected, or so she thought anyway. She settled into bed but found that she was having a hard time getting to sleep.

She picked up *Dread Lords of the Dragon Deep*, and soon she was engrossed in the world that Layla Scott Walters had built, despite the many typographical errors and the hard-to-read print. She finally drifted off wondering how in the world Sir Leonhart was going to get out of his latest scrape while separated from his dragon companion, Brietaster…

She rose, blurry-headed and in need of strong coffee, when Sam went around the house waking up everyone up for Christmas morning, as if he were ten again. But as she sipped her coffee and munched on a delicious flaky pastry, some of the fuzziness of her sleepless night wore off. She realized that a lot of her previous worries and sadness had melted away with the dawn. She was no longer upset about Peter; he was a buffoon. She was no longer even really worried about the glass ceiling that she had at her job in New York. Was she chained to that job forever? It seemed like a distant thing, barely real.

Then an inspiration struck her, something that had been germinating her head ever since she realized how much she was getting drawn into the book by that kooky author. Layla Scott Walters clearly had talent, but it needed nurturing. And much better presentation… most people wouldn't have Allison's patience for looking past *Dread Lords of the Dragon Deep*'s bad formatting and nonexistent editing.

So: what if Ben offered a publishing service at The Old Bookshop, in addition to selling books?

The bookstore could form partnerships with local authors, and sell those authors' books, and then also earn money from the authors to production services, such as printing, cover design, editing, and so forth. That would bolster The Old Bookshop's chances of survival. She could give Ben some advice about getting started; maybe even get directly involved with the process.

It wasn't a new model of business. Allison had come

across a few other bookstores who were incorporating similar services and flourishing because of them. There was one in New Hampshire, even, down in the Seacoast. She, or Ben, or both of them would meet with the owner of that bookstore to get some advice on running the publishing service. It'd be a great way to become a bigger part of the community, while at the same time diversifying the bookstore's income.

She couldn't wait to tell Ben about it. But she was also hesitant. She didn't want him to think she was trying to elbow her way into the business or to tell him how to run it.

Tread lightly. If Ben really did have feelings for her, he could still be in a dour mood from what he'd thought he'd seen. She'd have to tell him the truth about Peter first. Her own state of emotions toward Ben confused the matter further, though…

After the gift opening ceremony and all of the family's usual Christmas morning rituals, everyone sat around sipping coffee and hot chocolate, fiddling with their new presents. Allison had gotten Sam a book about the most haunted places in New England, and Christine a new pair of goggles to shield her from the sun during ski instruction. Allison's parents gave her the new generation of her preferred type of e-reader—they must have remembered that she'd cracked the screen on her old one—and Christine gave her a cozy mystery novel set in a town that suspiciously sounded like Holloway Green. Sam, to her surprise, gave her a bracelet that went so nicely with her cashmere coat. Maybe he'd had help from Sabrina in picking it out?

Christine sidled up next to Allison. "So I want to talk more about the second gentleman caller last night, not the first. Do you mind?"

"I don't know," Allison said, with a hesitant smile. "I don't know if there's anything there."

"Do you want there to be?" Christine asked. Before Allison could respond, she went on: "Ben is a great guy. But he might not wait around forever—you might have to make the first move. Last night might have been *his* attempt at a first move, but then he was scared off by that doofus Peter."

"That's true," she said. And then the words spilling out of her mouth surprised her. "I think I might actually be ready for something with Ben. Mom was right... I guess I really did need closure with Peter, and I certainly got it last night. He demonstrated to me everything I *don't* want in a man."

"How about what you do want in a man?" Christine asked. "How does Ben match up with that?"

Allison thought about the qualities she truly valued: honesty. Integrity. A good sense of humor. Generosity. Intelligence. She could associate every single one of those things with Ben Whitfield.

"He really is everything I want," she said. The sound of those words startled her, maybe most of all because of how true they felt. "Ben is amazing... but hold on. *I live in New York.* You aren't just laying an elaborate trap to get me to live back in New Hampshire, are you?"

Christine fluttered her eyebrows innocently. "Who, me? But seriously... if you *are* interested in him, these little complications have a way of working themselves out."

"Living six hours away is a huge complication!"

"Let's put it this way, then," her sister said. She took a meditative sip of her tea, then said, "If you never gave dating Ben Whitfield a chance, would you regret it? Yes or no, answer me quick!"

"Yes," Allison blurted.

"Then you need to go get that hunk of man," Christine said. "Do you see how it's as simple as that?"

"I do now," Allison said. Then she sighed. "But... I don't know, he sure seemed shaken to see Peter here. After he left, he apparently decided to put on this ridiculous all-night Christmas Eve sale at the bookstore. I drove down there last night, around two in the morning, and he was fast asleep with the door unlocked. So… what if he's a little crazy?"

"What if you're a little crazy too?" Christine said. "You'll be perfect for each other. You drove to a bookstore at two in the morning… I *thought* I heard someone sneaking around!"

Allison yawned without meaning to, thinking of her late-night drive. "Yeah, I suppose that's fair. But it can't be as simple as 'Go get him.' What does that even mean? Go find him and jump into his arms? He never even responded to my call or text!"

"Well, you know where to find him," Christine said. "The bookstore, right? And he must be awake by now."

"Okay," Allison said with sudden resolve. She got up and rushed to put on her coat and other warm things. "I'm gonna go over there right now. I'm gonna tell him how I feel. It's that simple, right?"

"Right!" Christine said.

But when Allison got to the bookstore, it was closed, and Ben was nowhere in sight. Through the front windows, she could see an addition to the store that surprised her: a massive, realistic model of a cog railway that looked much like the one that traveled up nearby Mount Lingonberry.

I do know where he lives, she thought to herself. She went down the block to the building that contained his apartment, above the general store, and knocked on the door. No answer there either.

She gave up, but returned later that afternoon, during the Christmas Day Festivities in the Square. Allison and her family, like most of the residents of Holloway Green, had a tradition of joining in the celebration after spending Christmas morning together, to catch up with neighbors and friends and brag about their gifts.

Just as she arrived at the event, she saw that Mayor Beaulieu was stepping up to the microphone. The mayor was wearing the crazy hat that she'd debuted at Meghan Whitfield's party.

"Merry Christmas," Mayor Beaulieu said, and that was the only worthwhile part of her speech, which droned on for much longer than the crowd apparently preferred. Allison saw a lot of restless folks around her. She realized that Ben had been right about the mayor—the speech was filled with empty platitudes and contained no real hope of change in the future, despite the tough economic circumstances.

Allison turned away, realizing that she'd let herself get distracted from the real reason she had come to the Festivities that afternoon. She had to find Ben and tell him about her idea to diversify the business.

She was excited to talk to Layla Scott Walters, as well, about the possibilities for her book. There wasn't much hope for her work ever being published by one of the big publishing conglomerations in New York, like the one she worked for. Somebody like Walters, without any connections or a pre-existing fanbase, would not be an attractive prospect. The big publishers favored books by celebrities and other clients whose existing platform would guarantee them millions of dollars in profit.

They said it was just business. But that part kind of stunk.

Local authors like Walters deserved more of a shot than the big publishers would ever offer them. Allison knew there must be many others out there like her, just in New Hampshire. She wished that the bookstore was open right now so that she could go over to the neglected LOCAL shelf, blow the dust off the books there, and take a look at them. She felt sure there were plenty of good stories in there waiting to be told.

She expected that, as with *Dread Lords of the Dragon Deep,* for many of these books their presentation would be lacking, and their editing would need to be spruced up. That was where the real opportunity lay for The Old Bookshop; it could be a local, trusted place to deliver those types of services.

Ben could hire a specialist to work on those services. Just one person could likely handle a range of the responsibilities, working without all the fluff and political bloat that a place like the publisher in New York would have. Someone with extensive experience in publishing and a strong desire to work closely with authors.

She had a candidate in mind for this specialist position.

But would Ben go for it?

CHAPTER 18

*B*en woke up with a caffeine headache in the bookstore as the light of dawn found its way through the front windows. He wandered blearily to the front of the store and discovered someone had done him the courtesy of locking up the bookstore; he turned and found a note tucked under a weighty historical thriller.

Merry Christmas, Ben. Thank you for coming by my parents' house, wish you could've stayed! Please give me a call when you're up. —A

P.S. Locked the bookshop door. Hope you weren't expecting anyone!

He frowned. He remembered being awake past midnight. Allison must have come by in the middle of the night, but why? Surely she hadn't been looking to take advantage of the sale.

She felt bad for you.

He waved away the self-pitying thought and grumbled. The store looked garish in the daylight with all the decorations illuminated. Sad, almost. Clearly an overnight Christmas Eve sale hadn't been a brilliant business opportunity after all. He hadn't sold a single book. All he'd earned from his idea was a bad night's sleep of a few hours at a hard wooden counter and waking up achy on Christmas Day.

He had to get going. He was supposed to meet up with Grandpa Skip, Meghan, and Sarah to exchange presents. He turned off all the lights, closed up the shop again behind him, and went over to his apartment to clean himself up and have breakfast. Just as he was drying himself off from the shower, the doorbell rang. Ben put on a towel and went to look out the front windows.

Below, on the street, the tall, white-haired figure of Grandpa Skip was waving at him. "Merry Christmas!" he shouted. "Get your butt down here!"

Ben dressed quickly and headed down the stairs to the street-level door. His grandfather was opening the trunk of his station wagon; he turned now to Ben and said, "Here it is! The great new centerpiece for the bookstore, finally finished!"

The model of the Mount Washington Cog Railway and Holloway Green looked stupendous in the full light of day. Ben applauded Grandpa Skip's masterful work. "Wow! This is perfect."

Grandpa Skip closed the trunk again. "I'm going to drive it down to the bookstore. Hop in, and then we'll figure out where you want to place it."

Ben agreed and got in the car for the short drive of just a block over. In all the excitement of installing the train model in the bookstore, and seeing the joy on Grandpa Skip's face, Ben didn't think about Allison until later.

He embraced the cold logic that the morning offered. He didn't have to worry about mooning over her anymore, now that she was back with her boyfriend again. It was Christmas; he wished them the best of the holiday season and all the happiness in the world, now that the madness that had inspired his all-night sale had receded. She deserved happiness.

Maybe she could change the guy and make him less of a jerk. *Yeah, right...*

When they were done setting up the model, Grandpa Skip turned to him and said, "So? What happened with Allison?"

"I did act on your advice. But it didn't turn out how I'd hoped."

Sheepishly, he told Grandpa Skip about visiting the O'Briens' house last night, how he'd seen Allison's boyfriend in attendance and then slipped and fell on the ice, spilling the chocolates, in his haste to escape from the property. He could at least laugh at his own hijinks now, with the benefit of some hours having passed since that painful incident.

Grandpa Skip laughed too. "That is a story, Mr. Ben. In any case, you gave it a shot, and I'm proud of you for doing so." His expression became thoughtful. "But I did see those messages you sent out about the bookstore's sudden 'all-night Christmas Eve sale'—what was your reasoning behind that, if there was indeed reasoning? You didn't *actually* stay up all night at the bookstore, did you?"

"No, sir," Ben answered. "I dropped off to sleep at the counter sometime after 1 am."

His grandfather sighed. "What possessed you to spend your Christmas Eve like that? Heartbreak? Or did you think you'd get some sales out of it?"

Ben had to look away. He felt his face getting red, in the true spirit of the season. "Okay, it was a little nutty. Maybe I needed to get my mind off Allison."

"How many books did you sell?"

He curled his index finger and thumb together and showed the goose egg to his grandfather. "Someone *almost* bought a book. If they'd felt a little more sorry for me, it might have happened."

Grandpa Skip shook his head. "Well, don't pull that kind of stunt again—you need your beauty rest! Please promise me you won't open the shop up again today. In fact, we should postpone the gift exchange with your sister and Sarah. We can do it after Festivities in the Square this afternoon. Go get some rest, Mr. Ben."

Ben nodded. "You're right."

"I'll come back this afternoon with Meghan and Sarah," Grandpa Skip said. "So, lock up, rest up, and I'll see you around three!"

On his way out the door, Grandpa Skip paused, looked back, and offered a final word of wisdom: "By the way, don't give up on love. You'll find it when you're ready."

Ben took a deep breath and said, "Thanks, Grandpa."

No, he wasn't giving up on love. He was just listening to the voice of reason. Whether or not the boyfriend was in the picture, Allison would have to go back to New York anyway after the holidays. And that would be that.

So Ben went back to his apartment, and since the revitalizing effects of his shower had worn off by now, he promptly fell asleep. He had dreams of someone knocking on the door, someone pounding away and trying to get in, doubtless inspired by his own misadventures at the O'Brien house.

When he was finally able to get up again, he realized it was mid-afternoon, and his stomach was grumbling loudly. From the noise outside his apartment windows, the big Christmas gathering downtown must be in full swing by now; he decided to go down and get some food there.

Festivities in the Square was an annual tradition in Holloway Green. As soon as Ben stepped out onto the sidewalk outside the apartment, he found himself surrounded by joyful fellow residents of the town, strangers and familiar faces alike, making a merry bustle to and from the town square. A little kid waved at him excitedly and said, "Merry Christ-mass!"

His spirits lifted and he returned the wave and the greeting in exactly the same intonation, emphasis on the "mass." *This town,* he thought. *This town will always be there for me, no matter what. Is there a greater place to live in the world?*

It had turned out to be a truly beautiful day, without a cloud in the sky. The temperatures were up around the low forties, making the snow and ice run in rivulets down the walks and gutters. Ben breathed in the fresh air happily. And then reality came crashing down.

It's Christmas. The deadline for reaching my sales goal for The Old Bookshop is today.

Had he actually made it to the goal? He had a sick feeling that he hadn't.

The numbers, he had to check the final numbers. He hadn't done the final calculations yesterday because he'd figured, stupidly enough, that he would have some sales from the Christmas Eve all-night event to add to the totals.

He headed back to the bookstore at a fast pace and let himself inside. The gigantic model of the cog railway train in the middle of the shop now seemed sinister, a stand-in for his grandfather himself. *Did you make your numbers?*

Ben went to the register and checked the final totals from both cash and card sales. His stomach dropped somewhere into the soil and granite far beneath his feet.

He *was* short. By several hundred dollars.

No. No, no, no.

"I have to make more sales," he gasped. Was it too late? It wasn't, was it? Grandpa Skip had to get back to Valentino Boggs about the offer tomorrow, not today. Grandpa Skip had said to make the goal amount *by* Christmas, not before Christmas. And sure, his grandfather had told him not to open up the shop again today, but surely Grandpa Skip didn't know that a few hours of operation today could mean the difference between success and failure for Ben.

He dashed around flipping on all the lights and then turned the sign on the front door to OPEN.

Stupid, to exhaust himself overnight and then waste so much of today. What time was it? He was supposed to meet Grandpa Skip at three.

He stared at the door. Maybe he should prop it open. It was a warm enough day, and he needed to draw people in from the Festivities. He strode toward the entrance, found a brick for the purpose he needed, and placed it in front of the door. A rush of cold air came in, making him shiver. He turned back toward the shop.

Then a soft, hesitant voice behind Ben surprised him. "Hi, Ben. Merry Christmas."

He turned to see Allison O'Brien on the sidewalk in front of the store, looking gorgeous, albeit like she hadn't slept well. *She must not have, if she came by to see me in the middle of the night...* To his dismay, his heart ripped open all over again. It was insensitive of her to show up like this unannounced. How could she rub her glowing presence in his face, when she must've guessed his real reason for coming to her house last night—on Christmas Eve, with a box of chocolates?

"To you as well," he said briefly. He ducked his gaze to avoid her eyes, concentrating on the townsfolk behind her. If only he could *will* them into the store…

She frowned at him, bobbing her head and trying to get him to look at her. "Ben, about last night. I want to explain to you, I—"

"There's nothing to explain," he said coldly. "I'm sorry for interrupting your family time, and especially when you had a visitor. Listen, I'm in a real bind. I have to make some more sales today or I'm going to fail to meet Grandpa Skip's challenge. So unless you're here to buy another book..."

Ben went back to the register. To his annoyance, she came inside and admired the train model, circling around it and viewing it from all angles. "Wow. This is amazing. It's the cog railway, right? And Holloway Green! Is this the work of your grandfather?"

"Yes—"

"Did he come up with this whole arrangement himself? I knew he was a model train enthusiast, but I never knew he was so masterful at creating them..."

He gave her a brisk, irritated look. "He's been working on projects like these for more than half of his life."

Her blue eyes glittered at him. Was it pity? "Ben, can I just tell you about last night, please? I tried to come to your apartment earlier, but no one answered. I, uh, came to the store late last night too, but you were asleep."

"I know. I saw your note."

"The guy you saw, we're not together anymore," Allison said. "I told you, right? Peter cheated on me. With multiple women, turns out. I didn't invite him to our house. He just showed up. And we kicked him out shortly after you left."

Why'd you let him inside in the first place, though? How did he know where your parents lived? Has he been there before? Ben flushed; this explanation about the boyfriend—the *ex*-boyfriend—wasn't as reassuring to him as Allison seemed to expect. It also didn't erase the fact that Ben had still run away like a coward. And the pratfall on the ice made it even worse.

"Last night was embarrassing for me," he said. "I don't want to talk about it anymore."

Allison looked taken aback. "Please, Ben. That wasn't—"

"Is there anything else I can help you with?" Ben said.

"There is," she said. She took a deep breath and continued. "It's something I've been mulling over the last couple days, but really came into clarity for me this morning."

"Oh?" Ben said with deliberate rudeness, hoping she would take the hint and go away. A young couple entered the bookstore and began to examine the new and notable fiction shelves. *Please buy something.*

"It's about the business," Allison went on. "Here's the concept: you could work with local authors and help to publish their books. Like the one who came in, Layla Scott Walters—she's actually a great storyteller. She just needs some help to show the gem of her story that's buried underneath a lot of bad presentation and editing. And I know there are a ton of other authors like her. Operating a publishing service through The Old Bookshop would give you an extra stream of revenue and diversify the business. And help ensure the bookstore's chance of survival in a tough economy."

"I've been doing just fine," he said.

"You could make a real connection with the community, be part of the larger literary scene in New England," she said. "I—I could help you get things started, with what I know about the business of publishing. I could create the position and work out the details. I know some great options to produce and publish books at a low cost, and could take on the steps that local authors are unwilling to tackle themselves. Make their products look professional, and so forth."

The idea did sound like it had merit, but he was doing his best to tune her out. She was probably just taking pity on him, anyway, after his embarrassing little show last night. He called out to the young people, "Let me know if I can help you find anything. Merry Christmas!"

"Ben?" Allison said.

"I appreciate your ideas," he said with cool professionalism, "and I will take them under advisement."

"That's it?" she said, sounding hurt and confused. "You know I've been doing this for a *living* for five years, in New York. The center of the publishing world. I know what I'm talking about—I can help you make this work."

He stared at her with angry impatience. "Ideas that work in New York, maybe they don't work up here. New York isn't the center of the universe, you know. And neither are you. I'm gonna do this on my own. Now please let me concentrate on actual customers."

She had no more words to say. She bit her lip and turned away, hurrying out of the bookstore.

He looked down at the register, aching with self-reproach and guilt.

Three o'clock arrived faster than it should have. Ben had made a few more sales by then, including a book that the young couple had bought, but it was nowhere near enough to close the gap. With a heavy heart, he closed up the bookstore and went to meet his family at the Festivities.

He spotted his grandfather over in front of one of the food stalls, ordering a couple of large bags of caramel popcorn for Sarah and Meghan, who were nearby. Ben waved at them and headed over, doing his best to bury the guilt that had been racking him ever since he'd turned Allison away.

He gave Meghan and Sarah big hugs and wished them a merry Christmas.

"We heard about the all-nighter you pulled," his sister said. "Are you out of your mind?"

"Maybe," he admitted. "Listen, Grandpa Skip, I ran the numbers. I failed. It was close, but I didn't meet the sales goal."

"I see." His grandfather's face turned solemn. "As you know, the deadline for getting back to Valentino Boggs about his offer is imminent. Tomorrow."

Ben nodded anxiously.

"And I've decided… to reject Boggs's offer," Grandpa Skip announced. "You have demonstrated that you have the verve, determination, and capability to make The Old Bookshop profitable. Forget about the numbers, Mr. Ben. A few days of sales can swing wildly in one direction or the other. What's important is the long game, and I already know you can do it."

Meghan and Sarah cheered. But Ben couldn't believe it. "Boggs was offering you a ton of money."

"It doesn't matter. I'm giving the first opportunity to buy the bookstore to you." His grandfather smiled. "Make me an offer."

Ben took a breath. "Okay, here's what I can pay for it," and he told Grandpa Skip the number that he'd calculated he could get away with that wouldn't involve too many soul-crushing loans.

Grandpa Skip nodded. "Done. Congratulations, Ben! We'll draw up the paperwork in the new year."

He opened his arms for a hug, and Ben hugged him hard. Ben's heart raced in his chest. He was thrilled! This was the best Christmas he could have ever imagined. Except…

His excitement was tempered by the fact that he'd pushed Allison away from him. He wouldn't get to celebrate the news with her. And why? Because of his poisonous jealousy. Whether or not it had a basis in reality, it was unacceptable.

"I have to find her," he said. "I, I treated her so poorly when I saw her today."

"Allison?" Grandpa Skip said.

"No, the Queen of England… yes, of course, Allison! I have to tell her the news. And beg her forgiveness, because she's got an idea that could make The Old Bookshop *so* much better."

"You go get her, then," his grandfather said with a wink. "I'm going to get Mr. Valentino Boggs on the phone and ruin his Christmas."

"But I've just met up with you guys," Ben said. "Are you sure that's okay?"

"Every one of these Festivities is the same, you won't be missing out," Meghan said. "We'll see you tonight. Go find your girl, Ben—it's time to open your heart."

But Ben didn't get far. As he weaved through the Festivities crowd, Sam O'Brien stepped right into his path. He was alone, without the girlfriend that Ben had so thoughtlessly insulted. With the season's premature darkness settling over the town square, Ben had a hard time reading his friend's expression. He hadn't forgotten how they'd last left things, so he proceeded with caution.

"Merry Christmas, Sam!" Ben said. "How has the—"

"Hey, what did you say to Allie?" Sam barked, skipping the pleasantries. "She was so hurt. Sounds like she had a great idea for your business, and you totally blew it off. She doesn't understand why."

"I'm going to talk to her about it," Ben said. He folded his arms, feeling his face burning, though whether from anger or shame, he couldn't tell. "I'll apologize. She… didn't send you to find me, did she?"

"No, idiot, I came to find you all on my own," Sam retorted. "I think I know the real reason you were such a jerk to her. Listen—the guy that showed up to our house last night, that wasn't Allison's boyfriend. Or at least not *anymore*. He's a total dirtbag who came up all the way from Manhattan because he thought Allie would be easy to win back if he just showed up."

"She told me," Ben said. "Why did you guys invite him

into the house, then? It sure seemed like she was giving him another chance, along with the rest of you."

"Allie needed *closure*," Sam said, accentuating the word oddly. "She needed to understand that he didn't care about her, and he made that plain within the first thirty seconds of opening his mouth. You would've seen it too, if you hadn't been a dumbo and you'd just stuck around. She was calling out to you!"

Ben's guard went up. His fear and pride had kept him from staying at the O'Briens' place long enough to listen to her—and now they were telling him to shut Sam out. "I was... I felt humiliated."

"Oh, boo hoo," Sam said. "You could have been a man and, like, not run away at the first sign of opposition. And then Allie *still* wanted to talk to you, today, and you wouldn't listen to her."

Ben bristled at this. Mostly because he knew that Sam was right. "You know," he said tightly, "you have some nerve to lecture me about dating, after you tried to make your sister set me up with Evie Desjardins without my permission, or Evie's."

"Yeah, why do you think I'm so frantic to talk to you now?" Sam nearly shouted. He ran his fingers through his downy beard, clearly agitated. "I'm trying to make up for that mistake. You need to talk to Allie *now.* She's going back to New York."

He sighed. "Yeah. I'm planning to. I have some good news to share about the bookstore with her, anyway."

"So, hurry up, then!" Sam was definitely shouting now. Passersby gave them both a wide berth. "When I said she's going to back to New York, I mean she's leaving for New York *right now!*"

CHAPTER 19

*A*llison fled the Festivities in the Square after Ben had so roundly rejected her, leaving the rest of her family there with only a hurried excuse. She drove back to the house and indulged in tears, but only for a few minutes before pulling herself together and pursuing the more civilized course of eating a bucketload of Christmas candy instead.

Then her phone rang. She almost didn't answer it—she didn't care if Ben had come to his senses and decided to apologize, it was *far* too late for that—but at the last minute she looked over at the display and saw that it was a New York number. The number of her demanding boss, in fact.

Ugh. Merry Christmas indeed.

"Hello?" Allison said with some reluctance.

"Allison. This is Jerry."

"I know. How is your hol—"

"Can you be here tomorrow?" her boss asked. Without waiting for an answer, Jerry continued: "I've already booked a flight for you from Logan Airport in Boston. It's leaving tonight at 10 o'clock."

"Well, you're not exactly asking me, are you?" Allison said, heat rising in her. "You're just telling me." But she found that she wasn't entirely surprised. She realized she'd been bracing herself for some kind of nonsense to crop up back at the publishing house and interfere with her vacation.

"I mean, it's a free country," Jerry said. "Absolutely, you can do whatever you want. But if you value your job? Then you will be down here when I'd like you to be down here. I'll see you in the office tomorrow at 9 am."

Allison considered fighting him on it. Then her shoulders slumped. She hated to leave her family with such little notice —she'd been hoping to ring in the New Year with them—but she knew she had no choice. "Can you tell me what this is about?"

"Yeah, so, Holmes is putting up some resistance to the round of edits that you suggested. And I thought you could talk some sense into him in person…" Her boss described the so-called emergency in more detail, as Allison's hackles raised. *All this to coddle an author, on the day after Christmas? It can't wait? Really?*

But in the end, Allison simply said, "All right, I'll see you tomorrow," and she hung up.

She fell back on the couch, rattled. If she was going to be able to catch a ten o'clock flight—from *Boston,* not Manchester, no less—she would need to leave the house, like… five minutes ago. This was so aggravating.

She reflected, though, after a minute, that this wasn't as aggravating as it *could* have been. If, say, Ben hadn't so thoroughly shot down her idea for the bookstore that he barely let her speak. Ah, the contempt in his eyes had been palpable.

Sure, he could hate the idea of working with local authors. That was fine, it was his decision. But he didn't have to be so *rude* to her. If he'd just…

"No," she said firmly, sitting up, "it wasn't fine for him to hate the idea!" She knew the concept had worked for other businesses. But he'd treated her like she was an amateur rather than the professional she was. Or, worse, like a stranger he just wanted to shoo away.

Allison heard the noise downstairs of her family coming back from the Festivities then. She padded down the stairs and said, "Hey, guys."

"Are you okay?" Sam asked. "You took off so suddenly."

"Yeah, I... tried to pitch Ben on an idea for the bookstore, but he wasn't having it," Allison said, and moved on quickly to avoid further discussion of that topic. "But there's something else. Mom and Dad, I'm really sorry, but I'm going to need to leave for New York earlier than I thought. Tonight."

"Tonight?" Dad asked. "Is it a work emergency?"

"My boss sure thinks it's an emergency, and that's the only thing that matters," Allison said.

Christine let out a gusty breath of indignation. "That's totally disrespectful to you. Making you get on a last-minute flight on *Christmas Day*... are you sure you can't just tell him to wait until the New Year?"

"I don't think my job would still be there in the New Year if I did that," she said. "I mean, not that I'm going anywhere in that company, but—I still have a tiny chance, I guess, and I don't want to screw that up."

Sam, who had seemed distracted to this point, now nodded in sympathy and said, "Man, I'm sorry. Just one thing before you start to pack up and everything—did you ever explain to Ben about what Peter was doing at the house last night? He might think that Peter was still your boyfriend or something."

"I tried," Allison said, "but he wouldn't listen to me. He was acting like a stubborn jerk. So I guess that kind of answers the issue in itself. If someone won't even listen to me, then they're certainly not ready to start dating me.

And... now I have to go back to New York immediately anyway."

"What kind of publishing business could they really need to get done the day after Christmas, anyway?" her sister Christine pressed.

Allison made a gesture of surrender. "It's hopeless to argue with my boss when he gets like this. I do need to ask you a favor, Christine. Would you be able to drive me down to the airport... like, soon? If not, it's okay, I can figure out another ride down."

"No, it's fine," Christine said. "The traffic's going to be a nightmare, but I'd be grateful for the chance to spend as much time with you as we have left, even if it's in a tin can surrounded by other tin cans. So what time do we need to leave?"

It only took Allison a few minutes to get all of her things packed up; turned out when her job was on the line, she could move more quickly than she would've expected. She had left a little room in one of her bags for her new presents, and she looked at them now and smiled, hit by an unreasonable desire to stay in her warm little hometown forever.

But there's nothing left for me here, is there? she said to herself. She was heading back to the glass ceiling that she couldn't seem to get out from under, but she supposed there were other job opportunities in the City to try for if she could get her motivation up... certainly more opportunities than around here.

A few minutes later, Christine had the car warmed up and ready to go in the driveway. Allison stepped through the curl of mist coming from the exhaust and and got into the front passenger seat. She switched off her phone in case Jerry decided to send her any more badgering messages. At least she could have this last time with Christine to chat before she got on her flight.

"So, sis," she said, "are you sick of Christmas music yet?"

"Never!" Christine announced. She pulled out of the driveway and onto the rural road.

"Actually, can we make a stop on our way?" Allison said.

"Sure, where to?"

A few minutes later they were pulling up in front of a small, tidy house on Lingonberry Lane. The windows were alight with the cheerful yellow glow of lamps. Allison hopped out of her sister's car and dashed up the front walk and knocked on the door. While she waited for it to open, she fished a battered envelope out of her pocket.

Evie Desjardins answered the door with Nicky attached to her right leg. She smiled at the sight of Allison, though her smile was a bit wary. "Hi, friend! Merry Christmas!"

"Yes, to you too," Allison blurted, shoving the envelope toward Evie. "It's… an old card I found at the house. I hope you don't mind the recycling."

"Of course not," Evie said. She opened the envelope and then turned the card over. "Oh… this is…"

"We were sixteen," Allison said. "You sent me this Christmas card when I was at one of my lowest moments. Brady Cote had called me a nerd and a dork and four-eyes, even though I didn't wear glasses! Somehow he'd found out I had a little crush on him and decided to be as cruel as possible in his rejection. And you said…"

"'I love you for who you are, Allie, forever and ever,'" Evie read from the card. "'You're gonna grow up and show Brady and all the other cavemen how cool nerds can be.'" A tear slipped down her cheek; she laughed quietly. "I don't even remember writing that…"

"Mommy, don't cry," said her son, reaching up for her as if to wipe her face, though it was impossibly out of his reach.

"Oh, sweetie, it's a happy cry," Evie said, sniffling. She pulled him up into her arms.

Allison was crying now too, though she kept knuckling at her cheeks to make the tears go away. *Silly old mess.* "That was, well, half a lifetime ago, but I held on to the card—it meant so much to me. I found it in my old room at my parents' house. Evie, it's so rare that a true friend comes along... among the millions of people back in New York, there's no one like you."

"I'm sure that's not true," Evie said, blushing. Then she noticed Christine's car, with Allison's bags visible through the back window. "Are you headed back there tonight? Already?"

She nodded. "It's a stupid last-minute work thing. But I didn't want to leave without saying I'm sorry, for trying to fix you up with Ben Whitfield. I know it made you uncomfortable, and I didn't..."

Evie held up a hand. "It's okay. It's okay, Allie. I know it was your brother Sam's idea, not yours. He came to see me the other day to apologize. He seemed very upset, thinking that he had caused a fight between you and me. But I'm not mad, Allie."

"You're not? You're sure you're not?"

"Positive," Evie said. "Again, I was mostly just confused because I thought you were leading up to saying that *you* wanted to be with Ben Whitfield. I thought you two would be amazing together. And then when you were helping him with the bookstore, it... well. It's too bad you won't be staying longer, but I totally get how work can be."

Ben and I could have been amazing together, she thought to herself. But she had to put a halt to that line of thought before the waterworks happened all over again.

She glanced back at the car. She really did need to head to the airport soon. "Evie, I promise I'm going to do a better job of being a friend from now on. You should come down to the

City with the kids this winter, there's a lot of fun things for them to do. I can show you around."

"I'd love that," Evie said, and wrapped her arms around Allison and held her for a moment. "Thank you, Allie."

"Thank *you,* hon. Merry Christmas." Allison waved goodbye and hurried back to the car.

CHAPTER 20

Sam's words made Ben realize that, yes, he had been an idiot. He'd been making too many assumptions about what would happen if he took a chance with Allison—just to protect himself. To prevent himself from being abandoned again, when in reality he was the one doing the abandoning. And now he was about to lose her forever.

He couldn't let that happen.

He rushed away from the town square, toward his truck. Sam had given him Allison's flight information just before he raced off. It was going to be tight, if not impossible. He needed to outrace Christine's car and get to Logan Airport in Boston before the sisters did, then intercept them at the terminal.

As he drove out of Holloway Green, he called Allison. Her phone went right to voicemail. He left her a message asking if they could talk. He sent her a text to the same effect. But if she had her phone off, she probably wouldn't get either the voicemail or the text in time. Ben's plans were coming down to catching her in person, never mind how much he dreaded the frantic drive that that would necessitate.

I've pushed someone away from me for the last time. His mind kept running through the times that he and Allison had spent together. Allison laughing and draping him with tinsel during the bookstore decoration. Allison under the mistletoe at Meghan's house, blushing. Allison in the horse-drawn carriage, with snow melting on her eyelashes...

He put some motivational music on the truck radio and headed to 16 South. Sam said that Christine and Allison had already hit the road, so Ben would have to speed to catch up with them.

Unfortunately, the flow of traffic slowed down as he went further south, running into snarls. He took advantage of little gaps in the press of vehicles wherever he could, but eventually the cars thickened into a standstill on the highway. Seemed like half the population of New England must have been returning from visiting their grandma or whomever for Christmas. Of all the luck...!

Growling in frustration, Ben steered his truck onto the shoulder and left it idling. He stepped onto the highway, wanting to take a peek down the line of cars ahead, heedless of the annoyed honking of the car behind him nosing forward. Then he realized he could spot Christine's car several cars down. It was distinctive, with that weird light purple color he had rarely seen in other cars.

At the sight of the car, he knew what he had to do. He ran along the shoulder, shouting, "Allison! Allison!"

He slipped, nearly fell—again. This time, Ben managed to keep his footing on the ice. It was too dark to see whether the occupants of the car had reacted to the shouts. The cars he passed were starting to move now as the traffic unclogged, and they were honking at the maniac running along the highway at night. Christine's car was moving too. They hadn't heard him!

He had to run faster to catch up with the car. He shouted out "Allison!" again.

This time, Christine's car slowed and then stopped, while the surrounding cars weaved around it and moved on, most of them still honking in outrage. Ben put a little more distance between himself and the passing cars, mindful of the risk he was taking. Finally, he came up alongside the front passenger window.

A pale smudge of a face peeked at him through the frosted window. Then the glass rolled down halfway. Allison gaped at him.

"Allison," he said.

"It's really you," she gasped. "What are you thinking, Ben?!"

"I've been a total monster," he said in a hurry. "I shouldn't have treated you that way. You tried to tell me that Peter wasn't your boyfriend anymore, but I wouldn't even let you speak."

She rolled down her window farther. "Well," she said, "that's true. You were definitely a monster. But thank you for saying so. We've got to get going, though... I have a plane to catch."

"Wait!" he burst out. He wished he could reach out for her right now, take her hand through the open window. "What if you stayed?"

"I... can't," Allison said. "I've got to go back down there for a stupid work assignment or my boss will fire me."

Would that be so bad? "What I mean is," he said, as inspiration and enthusiasm and love for her welled up in him, "what if you stayed in Holloway Green? To live? We could run the bookstore together."

"But I thought you hated my idea." She gave him a look that was somehow suspicious and hopeful at the same time.

Behind her, Christine let out a little noise and then stifled it. More cars swerved around them, blaring their horns.

"No, you were right. About the whole thing. It's a brilliant idea. And you'd be the perfect person to run the publishing service."

She looked thoughtful. "I don't know... That would be a big step..." But a brief smile played at the corners of her lips, before quickly receding.

"You said the people at your work don't respect you," he said. "That it doesn't look like you'll ever have an opportunity to advance. And look, your boss is even dragging you back down there on Christmas for some stupid reason. What if you've got an opportunity to advance *right here*? What if you bring a little New York to humble Holloway Green, and we all win?"

Allison's breath frosted in the cold. Her intense blue eyes studied him. "Ben... you've been carrying around a lot of hurt, for years. I didn't know until you told me. Are you sure you're ready to let me in? Ready to work with me so, um, closely?"

"I've been turning away from any chance to get close to people for my whole life," Ben said. "But I can't turn away from you. I need you with me, Allie. As my partner, as... as much and as deeply as you're willing to be with me. So now, I'm prepared to grovel. You deserve no less from me."

She gave him a wide-eyed look. "Oh, wait! What about Grandpa Skip? I thought you said you didn't make your sales goal, and so he'd be selling The Old Bookshop to Valentino Boggs."

"Turns out I came close enough for Grandpa Skip's satisfaction," he said. "He wanted to know that my heart was truly in it, that I wouldn't run away from Holloway Green anymore. The last several days proved that to him, so he's rejecting Boggs's offer and giving me the chance to buy it."

"But… do you really have enough money to pay him what the bookstore's worth?"

He gave her a tight nod. "I have enough money plus credit. I talked to the bank earlier this week. I'll be working off the loan for a while, but it's worth it. To help Holloway Green make a comeback. It means more to me than almost anything."

"Hm," she said. "I'd hate to see you saddled with long-term loans."

"It doesn't matter. If you… if you don't want to be romantically linked with a bum who's in debt, then you can reject that part of the deal. The two parts don't depend on each other."

Allison grinned at him and stepped out of the car. She started shivering as soon as the frigid night air hit her, and Ben wrapped his arms around her to lend her warmth. Snowflakes alighted on her hair, and color bloomed in her cheeks; she looked like a herald angel freshly landed on Earth.

"All right, Benjamin Whitfield. Let me explain how this is going to work," she said.

"Please do," he murmured.

"Because I've given it a lot of th-thought. You may or may not have noticed that when you were shooting down my idea out of hand."

He nodded. "I did notice. And I totally deserve that."

"We're going to be equal p-partners in this venture," she said. "Co-investors and co-owners. You run the bookstore with my help. I run the small press out of the bookstore with your help. Oh, and… I get to name the press. Just so you know."

He laughed, before giving in to a bout of violent shivering himself. "Sounds f-fair!"

"You're both nuts," Christine called to them through the window. "Please get in the car, for your own sakes!"

Allie fixed her brilliant blue eyes on him. Her face was quite close to his, but she didn't pull away. "But I have an additional condition that I need to insist on. I need to tell you the truth. It might complicate the business... it might make you want to retract your offer."

Ben felt worry stab him in the stomach. What could it possibly be? He said, "I'm standing here freezing my butt off on a dark highway in the middle of winter. What would scare me off?"

"Ben Whitfield, I've had deep feelings for you ever since we were teenagers. Especially when we were teenagers, in fact. That nerdy little Allison you remember from high school is still inside me. In fact, she might be the truest part of myself, more so than anything you see on the outside of me today. And before we get going on any bookstore business together, she insists on going on a proper date with you. You know, to fulfill the fantasy she's always had."

"So your condition for accepting the agreement," he said, "is to go on a date with me. And let your inner nerd loose." He grinned. "It's a deal."

He offered her his hand. She took it. Squeezed it hard.

"Ben, are you prepared to mix business with pleasure?" Allie said. "Because I foresee a lot more mixing in our future. Just know you won't be able to get away from me easily."

"I can't think of a reason I would want to anyway," Ben said. His heart was soaring.

"Good. That's very good." Now Allison closed her eyes and leaned toward him. He stroked her dark hair with his icy fingers and met her lips with his. And he realized he'd been wrong, what he'd been thinking when Grandpa Skip told him he could buy the bookstore. That had been great, but *this* was the best Christmas present he could ever have imagined.

The kiss went on for a long while. Honking erupted in a chorus behind Christine's car as angry drivers were forced to queue up all over again on the New Hampshire highway—but still audible above the din was the sound of Christine clapping, tears ran down her face.

"I love you both," she said. "Merry Christmas! Now please get in the car and we can get off at the next exit and get you a hot cocoa someplace. I don't think you all realize how much your teeth are chattering."

They all chuckled at that, and Allie went back into the passenger's seat while Ben jumped into the back seat. Then he jumped right back out again, laughing at himself. The bitter cold, and the excitement of the kiss, must have caused his brain to stop working for a minute there.

"I... need to get back to my truck! The keys are still in it!" he said giddily. He held out a hand to Allie. "Would you ride with me?"

"Go, go!" Christine said. "You two have a lot to talk about. Meet you at the next exit."

Allie accepted his hand with a broad grin. She stepped out of the car and into his life.

EPILOGUE

*A*llison, Ben, and Grandpa Skip collected a jovial little crowd to help them ring in the new year at The Old Bookshop and celebrate the business transferring to its new co-owners. Christine had brought Dell Gagnon and his mother with her. Mom and Dad were here, taking the night off from Jackpine Mountain. Sam had brought his paranormal-obsessed paramour, Sabrina.

Meghan Whitfield and her daughter Sarah were there too, along with Evie Desjardins and her young children. Teenage Sarah had been keeping an eye on Evie's kids, going through some coloring books with them and exclaiming over their cool toys, so that Evie could get a chance to relax and have a glass of wine and some snacks.

Evie clinked a glass with Allison. "To rekindled friendships and new beginnings."

"Cheers," Allison said happily. Then she glanced over at Frannie and Nicky, who had both abruptly passed out on the bookstore's couch in the corner. Sarah shrugged at Allison. "Oh no, I think they've had too much fun for one night."

"It is *way* past their bedtime," Evie concurred, "but they

insisted on coming along tonight. They love Grandpa Skip and they're so excited that The Old Bookshop is back open."

"As are we," Christine put in with a wry smile. "Just think, now Sam and I get to torment Allison year round instead of just one week out of the year."

The realization hit Allison afresh that she'd managed to resist the spell of New York City—she was still here in here hometown. The city hadn't managed to drag her back despite its best efforts. She wasn't going back.

She thought back to the very satisfying, albeit brief, phone conversation she'd had with her boss on Christmas night. She politely informed him that she would not be traveling down to New York City on a last-minute flight after all.

"I am about to start a new venture here in my hometown," she'd told Jerry as Christine drove them back north, through considerably less traffic than southbound. "Here in New Hampshire."

"Are you crazy?" her boss had said. "If you're not back in the office tomorrow morning, I'll fire you."

"I quit," Allison said. "You won't believe the opportunity I have here. It's going to be big. It's going to be huge, Jerry. Maybe we can talk about it someday."

"You really are crazy," her boss marveled. "You can't quit —I'm firing you right now! You're hereby fired, O'Brien."

"Too late," she said, grinning. "No hard feelings. I hope your Christmas has been very merry, Jerry." And she had hung up the phone.

She hadn't burned all her New York bridges, though. Valentino Boggs had taken Grandpa Skip's rejection with surprising good humor, and earlier this evening had even called Allison to congratulate her and Ben on buying The Old Bookshop.

"And I thank you, my pretzel," Boggs had said, "for introducing me to the charming community of Holloway Green. I may pursue further ventures in the town. May even settle there myself one of these days, if I can finally make my escape from this cursed City. For that I owe you gratitude. If you ever need any advice while running your new acquisition, please do not hesitate to reach out to me."

"I really appreciate that," she'd said. "But I have to ask, Mr. Boggs. Why do you keep calling me a pretzel?"

"Oh! I thought I already had." Boggs cleared his throat, then rumbled, "No offense was meant. Quite the opposite. You initially impressed me in the City not only with your diligence and determination, but your genuine love of and belief in the power of books. You stood out in a sea of empty strivers. The pretzel is an ancient, longstanding symbol for devotion in the Christian church—early Christians survived on flour, water, and salt alone during the time of Lenten fasting. Its shape evokes arms crossed in prayer. Your faith in the power of literature served you well at Bartleby-Flores-Bergman... may it sustain you in your new business, in the New Year."

So far, so good. Over the past few days, sales had been booming at The Old Bookshop. Even though the gift-giving season was over, people were more than willing to spend their new Christmas cash at the bookstore and add to their bookshelves. Some folks just wandered in off the street to get a better look at the huge model of the Mount Washington Cog Railway, and walked away with a book or two in their hands, new and happy customers.

And the new year promised even more bountiful returns when Allison started up the small press and publishing services through the bookstore. She was thinking of calling it Jackpine Press.

She'd already scheduled a meeting with Layla Scott Walters in early January; the author seemed thrilled to hear about Allison's interest in her hefty fantasy book. Especially when Allison geeked out about her favorite part, when Sir Leonhart turned down the title of lordship because it would have meant saying farewell to his best dragon friend forever. "Ah," Walters had said, "that's the very heart of the book!"

Ben drew near to her now, his warm brown eyes sparkling. He hugged her to his breastbone and kissed the top of her head. "I hope that this is an okay New Year's Eve date, Allie," he said. "I know we've been working a lot lately."

During their first date, the day after Christmas, they went to Antonio's Ristorante and ended up excitedly discussing all of their plans and potential options for the bookstore for the most part, rather than sweet nothings. But building the future of The Old Bookshop together was a romance in itself; they exchanged a lot of tender looks and kisses that night.

The new year would mean even more work, and a lot of challenges and risks. But it'd also be full of hope and new beginnings, that the two of them would experience together.

"I couldn't imagine a better New Year's than being with you," she said. "That's all I need. Well, and all these other beloved weirdos, of course."

"Of course." Ben got a startled look. "Oh! I have to start pouring the champagne for everyone so we're ready." He dashed over to the front counter and started pulling out glasses. She watched him grab a Santa hat and put it on too, which made her laugh.

She drifted around the bookshop floor, picking up bits of everyone's conversations.

"So the courthouse paid you actual money," Dell was saying to Sam. "Municipal money. From taxpayers' pockets."

"Yes, isn't that great?" Sam replied excitedly. "I'd love to get a couple more ghost-detecting gigs in the new year. Start making a name for myself."

Sabrina clutched his arm. "Isn't he dreamy…"

"He's something, all right," Dell remarked.

Allison moved on to eavesdrop on a conversation that her father was having with Grandpa Skip. The latter was excitedly showing Dad little details on the Mount Washington Cog Railway model.

"Aside from the questionable addition of Holloway Green, this train model seems very accurate," Dad said.

"Yes, the car and locomotive are true to the real thing," Grandpa Skip said with undeniable pride. "The mountain obviously isn't. That's Jackpine, not Washington. And the foliage, technically you wouldn't see all these types of trees in their full fall colors at the same time, so that's artistic license as well…"

Dell's mom was chatting quietly with Ben's sister over by the biographies and memoirs. Allison veered to a different direction and found Ben waiting for her, wearing his grubby Santa hat and holding out a glass of champagne to her.

She accepted the glass. "Thank you, Santa. Have I mentioned you're looking sharp tonight…"

"Maybe a time or two," Ben admitted. "Allie, we've got a big year ahead of us. But I just wanted you to know…" He leaned toward her.

"Yes?" she said, breathless at his handsome face so near.

"That year is starting in thirty seconds," he said. He turned up the volume on his Bluetooth speaker, broadcasting the New Year's Eve celebration live from Times Square in New York. "Do you wish you were down there with them?"

"Not at all," Allison said. "This is where I need to be. All right, this is it!" she added, in a louder voice to the rest of the party. "Ten! Nine! Eight!"

Everyone called out the rest of the numbers in sync with the broadcast, except for the kids, who were sitting up and rubbing their eyes in confusion at all the shouting. Allison said, "Happy New Year, Mr. Ben," and gave her newfound love a long kiss on the mouth.

When they finally came up for air, Ben said, "Hm. Usually only Grandpa Skip gets to call me that."

"A little advice," said his grandfather, grinning broadly nearby. Grandpa Skip planted a kiss on the cheeks of both Allison and Ben. "She gets to call you whatever she wants."

END

THANK YOU FOR READING!

Please leave a review for *Christmas at the Old Bookshop* online so that this book can reach a wider audience.

—Love, Augusta

ACKNOWLEDGMENTS

Thanks so much to my beta readers for their invaluable feedback: Michelle Boncek, Adrienne Bruno, Susan Deck, Jill Keller, Dea-Sue Pelletier, Chris Russo, Heather Thompson, Lynn Walters Rekhi, and Amy Wolfe. Their suggestions helped to greatly enrich this story and tie up a lot of loose ends.

Thanks also to friends who helped to brainstorm ideas for this book series: Krystina Bruce, Danielle Curley, Janie Dibble, Alice Gomstyn, Bobbiejo Hall, Jenn Knox Hastings, Tracy Hume, Shevani Jaisingh, Ariel Maloney, Megan Mattingly, Belle Morse, Meg North, Maren Tirabassi, and Trese Young.

The idea of an independent bookstore operating its own press came from RiverRun Bookstore in Portsmouth, New Hampshire (Piscataqua Press). Do check out the press's books as well as the bookstore itself!

Holloway Green can't be found on a map, but you may enjoy checking out northern New Hampshire towns such as North Conway and Jackson. The latter's family-owned Black

Mountain ski area was a loose inspiration for Jackpine Mountain. And the Mount Washington Cog Railway is real, of course!

Augusta St. Clair (a pseudonym)

New England, December 1, 2020

ABOUT THE AUTHOR

Augusta St. Clair is a New England author specializing in small-town sweet romance. Her name is a pseudonym. That means that Augusta St. Clair doesn't exist, but there's a real person behind the pen name who very much appreciates you reading this book. For more about books under the Augusta St. Clair name, please visit https://augustastclair.wixsite.-com/books

facebook.com/augustastclair

instagram.com/augustastclair

Made in the USA
Coppell, TX
07 December 2020

43667130R00132